I0619655

MECHA

ERIC S BROWN

SEVERED PRESS
HOBART TASMANIA

MECHA

Copyright © 2017 Eric S. Brown
Copyright © 2017 by Severed Press

WWW.SEVEREDPRESS.COM

ISBN: 978-1-925711-11-0

MECHA

The station's control center was functioning purely on reserve power. Its dim, red lights cast long shadows across the room as Chris sat staring out the forward window at the blue and green sphere beyond it. It was hard to imagine that every living soul on such a beautiful world was dead. The plague had blindsided everyone. There were rumors that it had begun in China but they were just that, rumors. The truth was that no one knew the origin of the plague. One day it just seemed to spring into existence and within a matter of weeks, it had spread across the Earth like an out of control wildfire. Health organizations struggled to find a cure as the world's militaries fought to contain it. Both failed.

Chris kept a calendar on the control room's main console. Each morning, he drew a line through another day and felt even more alone. He had been the only one aboard the Orb when the virus struck. The station couldn't be left unmanned and the time had come for a rotation in its personnel. He had drawn the short straw and agreed to stay on the extra few days until the next batch of scientists and astronauts could take over. Normally, the changeover would have taken place all at once, but issues groundside had made that impossible this go around so someone had to remain to watch over the station during the transition. Even now, Chris couldn't figure out if he had been blessed or cursed by being the one to stay.

During the early days of the plague at least, he hadn't been completely alone. There were other orbital stations and platforms like his. Their crews had kept in constant contact with him as they watched the world burn together. As time went on, though, many of them bugged out for Earth in search of their families, simply too afraid to go on alone among the stars, or out of a simple need to try to help those left below. Those who attempted to go home usually let him know of their plans before they made the attempt. Others he supposed took their own lives or something went wrong with the systems of the stations they were on because he never heard from them again.

On the upside, he was alive, and as far as he knew, that was more than could be said for any other member of the human race. On the downside, he was utterly, totally alone. All his recent attempts to reach anyone on the planet below had resulted in nothing but failure. He had monitored the news channels in humanity's last days, watching them fade away, one by one, until the airwaves only contained automated re-runs and snowy static. After that, he had tried the audio-only frequencies until they too were gone and even the cutoff and likely equally alone Ham radio operators were no more.

The Orb always maintained a large cache of supplies, enough to last its crew for a year or more. Chris had done the math and knew that since he was alone now there was enough to keep him eating well for far longer than that especially if he rationed what he consumed. Power wasn't a real issue either. He had cut power to almost all of the station's nonessential systems other than its Ki-land interface. That, he couldn't live without.

The only thing that kept him sane was Ki-Land. Ki-Land was more than just a game. It was a totally immersive world into which he jacked himself every day to escape the horror that real life had become. Ki-land had been created for personnel stationed on orbital platforms and space stations such as the one he currently commanded. It had been designed to help orbital personnel escape both the claustrophobic confines of their residence and the vastness of space. In Ki-land, off-duty personnel could visit their families, live out their fantasies, or even do something as simple as take a stroll through a lush green garden. Ki-land was, in essence, a world unto itself without limits or boundaries.

The use of Ki-land had spread into the civilian sector on Earth as time progressed, making real virtual visits with family and friends back home truly possible and no longer pure conjurations of the game itself. However, not even Ki-land was safe from the plague. As infected individuals on Earth jacked into its world, Ki-land had become corrupted by their presence. The taint of their madness had spread throughout Ki-land just as it had done in the real world below. Infected people who had jacked into the game before they died or died while from the plague while they were jacked in became monsters. Chris's character in the immersive world had originally been a soldier. Not much had changed from him except that now instead of battling it out with whatever enemy the world of Ki-land generated for him, he hunted the infected. It had become his mission in life to eradicate the infected monsters that stalked the various levels and regions of Ki-land. His holy war against the infected was his sole purpose for carrying on. He'd be damned if he let the plague claim Ki-land too as it had the Earth.

The very nature of Ki-land provided him with the allies and resources he needed to take on the infected if he could recruit them, but there were no cheat codes, psionic abilities, or magical wishes that gave him power over the game or its world. Everything he did took careful thought and real work just as it would have in real life. The game did give some advantages to its players, but they were slight ones and far from world-altering superpowers. Still, he had spent the last few months preparing for his big push towards clearing Ki-land of the infected once and for all. From his research both inside and outside of Ki-land, he knew there was a master reset switch hidden within the mechanics of the game that if he were able to reach would reboot the world into the paradise of fantasy it had been before the plague.

Chris shook his head, clearing it as he focused his attention on the things that had to be done for the day. He ran checks on the station's systems from its air scrubbers to its reactor to make sure everything was in the green and no maintenance needed to be done. After that was completed, he pulled himself along through the station's zero G corridors to scarf down a quick brunch of synthetic orange juice and egg substitutes before heading to where the Ki-land interface was located in the heart of the station. There were actually four, coffin-shaped gamer ports. Chris had cut power to the other three that weren't his own. Its interior glowed an eerie shade of green as he opened the port and climbed inside. The port's transparent, canopy-like cover closed above him as he stretched out and reached for the plugs to be inserted into the cybernetic implant points on his neck. A tingle of energy ran through his nervous system as he got himself plugged in.

"Activate Ki-land," Chris verbally ordered the port's A.I. as he settled in and his eyelids fluttered closed. At first, like always, there was only darkness and a void that appeared to stretch on into infinity and beyond. A small pinprick of light blossomed on the distant horizon of his perception. It grew, snowballing like an expanding supernova until it washed over him in a blinding flash.

****

Chris rolled about in the bed, its sheets tangled about him. His body was slicked with sweat as he groaned, flopping over onto his right side. The soft tips of Jordon's gentle fingers caressed the skin of his cheek.

"It's time to wake up, honey," she purred in a voice not much more than a whisper.

Chris grunted, fighting consciousness as she pulled him into it. He opened his eyes to see Jordon's face above him. Her blonde hair fell over her naked shoulders as her blue eyes met his.

"Ugh. Five more minutes," he pleaded despite the nightmare he had been having. His restless sleep had left him as tired as if he hadn't really slept at all.

"Not today," Jordon told him firmly. "General Aketo isn't the type of man you want to keep waiting."

At the mention of Aketo's name, Chris snapped fully awake. He lifted himself onto his elbows staring at Jordon. "That meeting is today?"

"It is." Jordon nodded leaning forward to kiss his forehead. "You'd better start getting ready for it too. You've waited a long time for this."

"You're bloody well right I have." Chris flashed a smile at her as he untangled himself from the bed's covers and threw his feet over its edge to touch the cool wood of the apartment's floor. As he started to stand up, he paused and looked back over his shoulder at Jordon. Her beauty was truly breathtaking.

5

"What would I do without you?" he asked.

"I have no idea," she said, grinning. "Now go save the world already."

Jordon followed him into the bathroom as he got into the shower.

"Do you think General Aketo will approve of your plan?" Jordon asked.

"He better," Chris answered, enjoying the feel of the water flowing over him as he shampooed his hair. "It very well may be the only chance we have."

Chris could tell Jordon was biting her lip as she asked, "We're still safe here, right?"

"No one is ever really safe," he reminded her as he finished up and stepped out of the shower into the towel she was holding ready for him.

Their military-issued apartment was located in New Busan. Unlike so many other places around the globe, New Busan had responded quickly to the outbreak of Hell on Earth when it had begun. Holding during those first days was more often than not the difference between whether a city fell or not. Those that had held had established perimeters and protocols to deal with the demon infestation to keep their citizens safe. Some cities like New Busan had fallen since those early days by simply being overwhelmed at their borders by invading demonic hordes, but New Busan was home to the center of power for Earth's remaining military forces. That wasn't to say it couldn't fall, but if it did, it wouldn't go easily. As yet, beyond a few skirmishes testing its defenses, the demons had made no real attempt at taking it. Though the demons grew in strength every day, Chris figured that an all-out attack on New Busan remained too costly for them to undertake.

"You know what I meant," Jordon replied, frowning.

Drying off, Chris swept her into his arms. "New Busan is a fortress, Jordon. If there's anywhere left in this gone to Hell world that's safe, this is it."

"I just worry," she whispered.

"I know," Chris said. "I do too. Nothing can last forever. That's why General Aketo has to approve my plan."

Jordon nodded, snuggling her head against his bare chest. "Then make sure you get him to," she urged him.

"I will," Chris promised her. "Then maybe … just maybe …We can all start over again."

Chris headed back into the bedroom, donning his uniform as Jordon stood in the bathroom doorway watching him.

"It'll be okay," he assured her again. "You'll see. You just stay safe while I am gone."

"And you be careful out there you." Jordon looked on the verge of tears. "If you don't come back to me …You're all I have left, Chris."

"Ditto," he said with a laugh, trying to cut the tension between them. It worked.

"You jerk," Jordon shouted and threw the wet towel she had collected from the bathroom floor at him as she followed him out of the bedroom.

Chris narrowly dodged it. "See you soon, love." He laughed and then gave her a final kiss before leaving her standing in the living room as he headed out its front door into the hallway beyond it.

****

General Aketo sat behind his desk as Chris entered his office. The general was scanning over a stream of data on the pad he held. He looked up at Chris with a concerned expression.

"Good to see you're on time for once," General Aketo said.

"You don't pay me for my punctuality, sir," Chris replied, smirking.

"Have a seat." The general gestured at the chair opposite from him.

Chris sat down as General Aketo handed him a data module interface.

"Take a look at that," he ordered.

Plugging the data module's extended cable into the interface point of his right wrist, Chris flinched as its contents poured into his mind.

He watched as a large group of soldiers located at Grid Delta on the outskirts of New Busan came under attack. From beyond the rows of barbed wire, machine gun emplacements, trenches, and observation towers that composed Grid Delta's defenses, wave after wave of demons poured towards the soldiers. Machine guns blazed, spraying the night with streams of death as orange tracer rounds streaked through the darkness. RPGs and cannons fired. A heartbeat later, explosions ripped into the masses of demons. Body parts and splattering blood flew skyward. Chris saw a demon with the legs and lower body of a spider and the top of half of a man with pincers for hands take a burst of automatic fire to its torso. Its chest ruptured as the bullets pounded into it. The demon shrieked as it collapsed with the white of bone protruding from the mangled meat around its sternum. Another demon with the body of a man and a head that resembled a cross between that of a ram's and a dog's was caught in the shockwave of a grenade that detonated behind it. Shards of shrapnel pierced the monster's back, blowing through its body to leave gaping exit wounds in their wake. The carnage continued as the demons fought for every inch they gained towards Grid Delta's defensive line. The demons paid no heed to their brethren that died around them in droves. Their burning eyes, a sea of red, yellow, blue, and green glowing orbs, remained focused on their goal ahead of them.

The soldiers kept up their grisly work, reloading to commence firing again as soon as a weapon was emptied. For all their efforts, however, the demons edged closer to the defensive line with each passing second. The rolling tide of their numbers simply could not be stopped. One soldier, apparently desperate and determined not to let the line be broken at any cost, hopped into a hover jeep. It shot upwards several feet into the air as the blades that roared to life. The Jeep flew forward to meet the front wave of the kaiju attackers, plowing into them. As the jeep smashed into the demons, the soldier's thumb came down hard on an activator switch that sent an electrical current into the load of explosives the jeep was carrying in its rear. The explosion lit up the night like a miniature super nova. The blast swept close to a hundred of the demons away in a rush of heat and flames, sending the demons back to whatever Hell they had crawled out of. The soldier's brave sacrifice bought the other defenders on the line a few precious seconds to get their breath and recover from the demons' relentless onslaught. It might have been enough to turn the tide of the battle had the very ground itself opened up beneath of the center of Grid Delta's line. A large patch of the ground spanning at least thirty feet across and twenty feet wide exploded upwards as a writhing mass of slime-smeared, barbed tentacles emerged to grab at the soldiers around it. Men screamed as they were plucked up and crushed in the grip of the tentacles. Many of those lucky enough not to be ensnared by the groping tentacles were knocked from their feet and slapped aside. All looked to be lost and the defensive line of Grid Delta broken as the tentacles took their deadly toll on its defenders but then, everything changed.

From the rear of the defenders' position, three, tall metallic forms appeared. Their armor gleamed in the starlight and flashes of weapons' fire as they advanced toward the demons. Chris recognized them at once. Their names were Blazing Bushido, Juggernaut Wrecker, and Staggering Firepower. Staggering Firepower raised its arms as they unfolded into twin clusters of multi-barreled machine guns. The mecha opened on the advancing demons still approaching the line with a continuous booming thunder of automatic fire. Demons died by the dozens as Staggering Firepower mowed them down, their bodies being chopped to bits and pieces by the barrage of high-velocity rounds that tore through them. The twelve-foot-long blade of the katana Blazing Bushido carried spouted flames that ran along its length from top to bottom as the mecha threw itself at the mass of giant tentacles. Blazing Bushido danced through the tentacles, springing from one cluster of the grouping limbs to the next where they emerged from the ground, slashing and hacking at them in a berserker-style fury. The mecha moved with near unbelievable grace as its blade severed the tentacles sending splashes of foul, black blood flying. Juggernaut Wrecker wasn't about to be shown up by the other two mecha though. She charged forward in the oncoming kaiju as Staggering Firepower lifted her arms towards the sky to let her system reload them. Juggernaut Wrecker was just as unstoppable as her name implied. Her hammer like fists caved in demon skulls and plunged through scales and chitin alike, leaving a trail of monstrous corpses in her wake.

The demons must have known they were beaten because as quickly as they had appeared, they turned tail and ran. Demons skittered, slithered, and sprinted away from Grid Delta's defensive line. Staggering Firepower killed dozens more of the monsters during their retreat before the night finally fell quiet and the battle was truly ended.

The stream of images flowing into Chris's mind came to an abrupt halt and his eyes popped open as he sucked in a startled breath. As he took a moment to recover, he noticed General Aketo staring at him.

"Before you ask, Chris," General Aketo said, "yes, it's that bad all over, not just at Grid Delta. The demons have finally started to really come at us. I've had to deploy mecha squads at most of the Grids around New Busan. That's why I wanted you to see that so that you would understand what we are up against at the moment."

Chris removed the cable of the data module from his wrist, handing the device back to General Aketo. "I had no idea, sir," Chris said. "But ..."

"Don't 'but' me Chris. Not after what I have just shown you," General Aketo warned. "You know fragging well before you ask that I can't give you what you want."

General Aketo paused for a second, still glaring at him, and then continued, "We're not the only ones hurting either, Chris. We've lost all contact with the two remaining city forts in the United States. The one in London is barely hanging on by a thread, and Australia ... Well, they're holding just fine, but you know we can't count on them for any sort of help if we get desperate. They had become isolationists even before the demons entered Ki-land."

"I understand all that, General Aketo," Chris started, chose his words carefully. "I really do. I still think the only shot we have is going on the offensive though. If we continue to just try to hold out like we are, that's a death sentence for every man, woman, and child in New Busan, maybe the rest of the world too."

"I know you believe there is a centralized force that can be used to stop all this, Chris. I've read your reports on it. The sad truth is you have no real proof to back up your theory. Even if you did, after seeing what I just showed you, tell me, do you really think I can spare the mecha to give you the kind of assault group you'd need to reach it, much less take it?" General Aketo asked him.

"With all due respect, sir, taking the Nexus is our only hope," Chris argued. "The Hexer and Psi guilds here in New Busan have pretty much stayed out of things so far. Couldn't you draft them into service? If you added some of their members to the Grids, it might free up enough of our mecha—"

"Stop it, Chris," General Aketo ordered him. "There is no way I can force the Hexers or those Psi freaks to do anything they don't want to. The Hexers have turned all their focus into making their guild headquarters into a trans-dimensional safe zone, whatever the heck that means. And the Psi guild here in New Busan is little more than a joke. Their membership is less than a hundred and most of them nothing more than low-level empaths at best. Regardless, they are private organizations and outside of my jurisdiction even given the current state of martial law."

Chris sighed but refused to be defeated. "There has to be a way, sir; something we can do other than just sit here waiting to die when the defensive Grids are finally overrun."

"Then you'll have to find it on your own because my hands are tied," General Aketo told him. "Defending New Busan and keeping its populace safe is and has always been my primary duty. I can't do that and give you what you're asking for too."

"And that's your final answer?" Chris pleaded.

"I'm sorry, Chris, but yes, it is," General Aketo replied sadly. "New Busan comes first over everything else."

"You're making a mistake," Chris said, leaning forward in his chair.

General Aketo shrugged. "I'm releasing you from your duties, Chris. Go home and spend some time with Jordon. I give you my word that I'll keep the demons at bay as long as I can. Who knows, this new push of theirs may be nothing. We've fought them off before."

Chris kept his seat, staring at the general, trying to hide his anger and hoping that Aketo might yet change his mind.

General Aketo cocked his head at Chris. "Did I not make myself clear, soldier? You're dismissed and off active duty until further notice."

"Yes, sir," Chris snapped as he got up and left the general's office.

****

As he walked through the busy corridors of the defense center, Chris looked for somewhere to get out of the crowd so he could tap into Ki-land's player interface. At last, he spotted a door labeled closet. Trying its knob, he found it to be unlocked. He let himself into the small room, shutting its door behind him. Chris raised his wrist, concentrating on it, until a control bracelet shimmered into view on it. The bracelet wasn't real. It didn't need to be. Nothing in Ki-land truly was. There was no need for his interface to appear as a bracelet either. Chris had grown up on eighties pop culture and just liked his interface to appear that way. It helped him focus on it.

Chris's fingers danced over the control keys on the bracelet conjuring into existence an avatar of the master A.I. that ran Ki-land.

"Good afternoon, Chris," the glowing, metallic face of Ki said, beaming at him. "How may I help you today? Are you enjoying your gaming experience?"

"Ki, I need you to display a real time image of Breaker Bay 2," Chris ordered the A.I.

The floating image of KI's face changed, spreading out in the shape of a flat screen which displayed the location Chris had ordered it to. There were a total of eight Breaker Bays in New Busan positioned around the city in such a way that every part of the city could expect fast coming aid from one the bays should it be needed. And all eight bays were stationed as close to the city's defensive perimeter in regards to their location as possible too. Each bay contained between four and a dozen mecha with at least half their number always on alert for immediate dispatch. Breaker Bay 2 was where Chris's personal mecha, Chimera Overkill, was stored. Chris watched the bay's techs working on his suit, making sure it was battle ready. Three other mechas stood alongside in the bay, towering over the workers, techs, and security personnel below them.

Chris couldn't believe he was actually thinking of stealing Chimera Overkill from New Busan's defense forces, but General Aketo had left him no other choice. Just stealing his own mecha wasn't going to be enough though, even if he pulled it off. He was going to need help and not just with getting out of New Busan. The Nexus was half a world away and that world was ruled by the demons. How the infected had become known as demons inside the game of Ki-land, he didn't remember or care, but the name fit perfectly. The digital spectres of those who had gotten infected in the real world and had carried the effects of the plague into it with them were the epitome of all things monstrous, chaotic, and evil. No two demons were alike. Some were giant, kaiju-like abominations that stalked Ki-land, leveling entire cities in their wake and others were human sized, though there was little else human about them. Demons came in every shape and size and each had their own means of killing anything human they encountered. Just as in the real world, the infected in Ki-land sought nothing but violence, blood, and death … and with each PC or NPC they killed in the game, their numbers grew and their infection spread.

The super suits known as mecha were the only sure way to stop them. The creation of mecha inside the game on the level that they existed now had come about almost at the same time as the birth of the demons when the infection spread from the real world into Ki-land. It was almost as if the game's controlling A.I. had nudged the game into creating them as adversaries to the demons. That wasn't to say that the more powerful Hexers and Psionicists couldn't slay the demons too; heck, even enough conventional weaponry could kill a demon if enough damage were inflicted to it, but nothing matched the sheer destructive power that mecha could deliver.

Chris sighed and shutdown his virtual window into Breaker Bay 2, ending his interaction with Ki. Beyond providing him with knowledge he wouldn't otherwise have if he were a mere NPC, Ki could do very little to help him. Chris knew he needed help; the question was simply where to get it. The mecha pilots of his squad were loyal to him and would follow his lead if he asked them to accompany him to the Nexus, and four mecha were a heck of a lot better than just his own, but they were still going to need a means out of New Busan other than fighting their way out. Chris didn't doubt for a second that General Aketo would send other mechas after him and his squad if they tried to take their suits and leave. He had no desire to fight other mecha pilots or worse, endanger the city itself by damaging or destroying any of its defensive mecha force on his way out. New Busan needed every mecha it had, and he would already be leaving it with four fewer than it currently had if he really did have the balls to carry through with the plan forming in his head.

No. What he needed was a Hexer or a Psionicist who could either open a doorway out of the city or mask the departure of his squad as they left. Chris hated Hexers. He had never been a fantasy genre sort of player. He understood that magic had its own rules just like tech did, but they made no sense to him at all. As much as he hated Hexers though, he wasn't afraid of them like he was Psionicists. A Psi could get into your head. There was no hope of keeping anything secret from them if they wanted to know it. Worse, the most powerful of them could do nightmarish things to even the mind of a Player Character up to and including taking it over or wiping it entirely, leaving nothing but an empty void where thoughts, emotions, and memories once existed. Chris shuddered and made his choice.

He left the Defense Center, flagging down a cab on the street outside it. As the driver pulled up to the curb for him to get in, he opened the cab's rear door, sliding into its backseat, as he said, "Take me to the Hexer Guild Headquarters."

The driver shifted about in his seat to look through the thick pane of glass that separated them.

"You sure about that, buddy?" the driver asked with a look of concern.

"You heard me," Chris nodded.

"That'll be triple the normal rate then," the driver said matter-of-factly.

"I'm good for it." Chris flashed the driver his mecha pilot ID.

The driver's eyes went wide. "I'll say you are!" he exclaimed, seeing the ID card. "Mind telling me what a mecha pilot wants with the Hexers?"

"That's classified," Chris growled. "Now shut up and drive."

"Yes, sir!" The driver turned back around in his seat, getting re-settled behind the cab's steering wheel. The cab lurched as the driver kicked it in gear and it shot out into traffic moving as fast the road conditions allowed.

****

The cab pulled over at the curb. Up ahead was a sealed-off block section of New Busan that belonged to the Hexers' Guild containing their headquarters. The building behind the barricade of barbed wire fence was literally glowing.

"That's it, buddy," the cab's driver said to Chris. "Mecha pilot or not, I can't get you any closer."

"Thank you," Chris told the driver, handing him his credit chip. The driver swiped it and passed it back to him.

Chris got out of the cab, watching it pull out onto the road and disappear into the midday traffic before turning towards the guild headquarters. He started walking towards it. As he did so, he noticed that despite the barricades, there were no guards. Chris made his way through them, approaching the building. He felt a tingling sensation as he started up the steps to the building's main entrance. The feeling of it reminded him of walking through a spider web. He knew that the Hexers were a paranoid lot and that they used protection spells on their places of residence. Since this was their communal headquarters, it made sense they would do the same here, especially given that supposedly almost all the Hexers in the city had supposedly moved into the place on a permanent basis.

Reaching the door, Chris paused to examine it. There was nothing otherworldly or out of the ordinary in its appearance. The door looked to be made out of a thick, heavy wood. As he reached out to take its knob in his hand to see if it was locked, the door swung inward of its own accord. A freckled young woman dressed in loose blue robes that sharply contrasted her red eyes moved into the doorway, blocking his path.

"Colonel Avalon?" she asked, sizing him up as she looked him over.

Chris nodded. "Yes, that's me. How did you know …?"

"We try to keep a close eye on those who would seek our aid," the young woman explained. "You are expected. Master Travi is waiting on you in his personal sanctum."

"Right," Chris stuttered, unnerved and caught completely by surprise by the unexpected welcome.

"If you would follow, I shall take you to him," the young woman told him.

"And who are you?" Chris asked as he followed the young woman through the building's foyer and to a flight of stairs that led upwards to the floor above.

"My name is Kristen. I am one of Master Travi's apprentices," the young woman answered.

"So you're not a Hexer then?" Chris tried to keep from thinking about how radiant and beautiful Kristen was. Her pale skin and the grace with which she moved didn't make it easy. He knew she wasn't a psionicist, so he doubted she could read his thoughts, but it was better to be safe than sorry later.

Kristen chuckled as she smiled over her shoulder at him. "Oh, I am a Hexer, Colonel Avalon," she said, "but I have a long path ahead of me to becoming a master."

The very walls around them as they walked seemed to shimmer and vibrate with an unexplainable energy. Kristen didn't appear concerned by them so Chris tried not to be either as they continued up the stairs.

At last, they came to a massive set of wooden doors and Kristen stopped in front of them. "This is Master Travi's sanctum. You have but to knock in order to enter. I'll leave you to your business with the master, Colonel. May the spirits shine upon you and be with you in all that lies ahead."

Kristen gave him a half bow and then left him alone in the corridor outside of the massive doors. Chris took a moment to collect himself and his thoughts before he raised his hand to knock on them. When he did, they parted before him, moved by some unseen force to allow him entrance. The room behind them was a large one. It was spacious with a high ceiling that curved in a sort of half circle. A lone figure sitting cross-legged hovered in the air above the floor of the otherwise empty room in its center. The figure was cloaked by the deep shadows of the room as the only lights within it were a handful of candles that burned and flickered at random intervals along its walls.

"Master Travi?" Chris ventured, starting towards the man in the room's center.

"Colonel Avalon," Master Travi answered him, opening his eyes as he emerged from the trance-like state he had been. He uncurled his legs as if stepping off an invisible platform onto the room's floor. "You've come seeking help in your quest, have you not?"

Chris stared at Master Travi. The master Hexer was barely older than he was based on the sound of his voice, the smoothness of the skin of his exposed hands, and the midnight blackness of the long hair that crept out of the sides of the hood obscuring his face.

"I am not reading your mind if that's what you are wondering, Colonel," Master Travi assured him. "The spirits foretold your coming on this day."

"What else did they tell you?" Chris asked, trying not to sound as skeptical as he felt.

Master Travi pushed his hood back allowing it to fall onto his shoulders. His features were angular and shaped like those of a bird. Master Travi wore thick, bottle-shaped lenses over his eyes. His lips were thin and tight about his mouth. Were it not for the "mystical" style of his clothing, Chris might have pegged the man as being an IT tech or some other type of techie nerd.

"They tell me that you seek the Nexus, the very heart of Ki-land, and the power that resides there," Master Travi replied, smiling.

"I do." Chris nodded. "I believe the Nexus is the only means of stopping the demons before all of Ki-land falls to them."

Master Travi smirked. "And you would be correct in that assumption, Colonel. The headquarters of our guild in which you are standing is the last of such headquarters in all of Ki-land. Our brothers and sisters around the globe have already fallen to the demons. We, here in New Busan, are the last of our kind."

"I … I wasn't aware of that," Chris said. "I am sorry for your loss."

Master Travi waved a hand dismissively. "All things pass in time. We magic users are no exception to that universal truth. Perhaps we are passing onto the next level of existence prematurely, but if that is true, then we have no one to blame but ourselves. We should have foreseen the coming of the demons and been ready for them."

"No one saw the demon plague coming." Chris frowned. "And even when it began, no one really believed it was as deadly as it is."

"The failure of others does not excuse one for making the same mistake." Master Travi matched Chris's frown with one of his own. "But none of that matters now. What's done is done. We can only continue along the path the spirits have set for us and do what we can to survive it."

"And that's why all of you that remain have gathered here?" Chris asked.

"Yes," Master Travi confirmed. "Many of the remaining masters believe that our only hope is to bunker down and shield ourselves until the plague has run its course and time washes the demons away from Ki-land, as it does with all things."

Master Travi gestured at the walls of the room they stood in. "Most of us spend the bulk of our waking hours working on this structure's defenses. Spells upon spells are layered on and about these walls. Should the demons assail this place, it is our hope that they will find it impenetrable."

"But you don't feel that way, do you?" Chris met Master Travi's eyes.

"I do not," Master Travi admitted. "I believe all this is a waste. No matter how strong these walls are, when the demons arrive, they will break them, and we will have no choice but to flee to another world or another time in order to escape death at their claws."

"And that's why you allowed me this audience with you," Chris said.

Master Travi nodded. "I believe as you do, that the Nexus is the key to stopping the demons. What I do not know is how. The spirits whisper to me and me alone that you are the answer to my question, Colonel, and that perhaps you are the only hope for us all."

"Does that mean you'll help me then?" Excitement and hope grew in Chris as he stared at the enigmatic Master Travi.

"I will." Master Travi grinned. "Only one other Hexer believes as I do among all of us that remain, but we two will do all we can to assist you in reaching the Nexus."

"Who is the other?" Chris asked.

"You've met her already, my good colonel." Master Travi laughed. "She led you to me."

"Kristen?" Chris was taken aback. "But she said she was just an apprentice."

Master Travi appeared insulted by his remark. "Kristen is well on her way to becoming a master, Colonel, and already a full-fledged Hexer in her own right. Besides, you are in no place to turn away anyone who would flock to your banner. Now go and gather those of your squad. The two of us will be there when you need us. You have my word on that."

"Thank you, Master Travi." Chris half bowed as he had seen Kristen do earlier to him and then turned, leaving the master to his meditations. He knew he could count on what Master Travi had told him as the truth. When a Hexer gave their word, they were bound to it by the same spirits that they claimed their magic came from.

****

"… And that's my plan," Chris finished, glancing around at the three people he shared the table with. Their expressions were a mix of confusion, fearfulness, and amazement. There was even a trace of anger in Brannon's. That was to be expected though. Brannon was as a "by the book" guy as could be.

"Let me get this straight, sir," Prince said, leaning forward in his seat. "You want us to steal our own mecha from New Busan's defense force, desert our posts, leave our friends and family behind, and travel halfway around the globe to find this Nexus thing so that we can use it to stop the demons once and for all?"

"That's about the size of it." Chris did his best to give a confident grin.

"I'm in!" Prince laughed, flopping back in his chair with a wide smile stretching his lips.

"You would be," Brannon growled at Prince.

"I don't get it, sir." Caroline frowned, ignoring the other two. "What makes you think this Nexus thing can really stop the demons?"

"I'm afraid you're just going to have to trust me on that one, Caroline," Chris answered. There were a few NPCs that understood that the world they were a part of wasn't the real one, but they were rare and often not human in some manner. Chris wasn't about to go into the nature of Ki-land with the other three members of his squad. To them, Ki-land was the real world and the only one they had ever known. The less they knew about it being just a game, the better. If he told them, they would likely either flip out and have some kind of breakdown or report him to his superiors as so being so insane that he needed a straightjacket and a padded cell to call home.

"What you're asking of us is wrong on so many levels colonel that I don't even know how to put my feelings about it into words," Brannon said, sneering at him. "Even if this Nexus thing can do all you say it can, there has to be another way to carry out your plan without betraying everything we hold dear in the process."

Chris shook his head. "I've tried talking with General Aketo, Brannon. I really have. The man just won't listen. He'd rather sit here and wait here to be overrun, as we surely will be one day, than think outside of the box. I *know* that the Nexus is the only hope we have of cleansing Ki-land of the demon plague and returning things to how they were before the monsters came with every fiber of my being."

"But how do you know?" Brannon pressed him.

"Again, you guys are just going to have to trust me on that part if we do this," Chris answered, sighing.

"Roger that, Colonel." Caroline nodded. "Your word has always been good enough for me. You can count me in too no matter how crazy all this seems."

"Great! So that just leaves me as the voice of reason then huh?" Brannon scowled at the others.

"Spartans stick together, man." Prince eyed Brannon. "It's what makes us who we are."

Sparta Squad was the name of their mecha unit. They had all agreed on the name when Chris had taken command of the squad when it formed. All of them liked to think of themselves as warriors of the highest order, and in truth, they were. To get into Sparta Squad, one had to be among the best of the best. It was one of the last three super mecha units left in the world. Their suits weren't the average-line defender models. They were giants designed to take on the worst that demonkind could throw at the city. Duking it out with demons that could level a skyscraper with a swipe of their tails was old hat for them.

"Look, Brannon," Chris pleaded. "I know how wrong all of this is, and I know I am asking a lot of you, but if we don't do this, then Ki-land dies. It's as simple as that."

Brannon removed a cigarette from the pocket of his jacket and lit up, taking a deep drag from it.

"I don't like this, Colonel. I don't like any of it," Brannon said.

"I'm not asking you to like it, Brannon," Chris said. "I'm asking you to step up and help save the world. So are you in or are you out?"

Brannon blew out a mouthful of smoke and then took another deep drag that consumed nearly half of the cigarette he held as Chris stared at him waiting on an answer.

"Fine. I'm in," Brannon said at last, "but I want your orders about all this in writing. If we pull this off and there's a world left for the crap to hit the fan in afterwards, I want to be covered legally."

"Come on, man, if there's a world left, we'll be heroes!" Prince nearly shouted which made Chris thankful that the bar he had chosen for this meeting was almost empty. Even so, a few of the other patrons glanced at their table in response to Prince's outburst.

"Keep it quiet, Prince," Chris warned him. "We don't want the whole world knowing what we're up to."

"Clearly, you're not a Ghostbusters fan," Brannon said to Prince. "They saved the world and look how things turned out for them."

Chris couldn't help but smile at the movie reference. The pop culture of the real world was deeply ingrained in Ki-land too. The game's players had brought it into the world during its early days just as the infected had brought the demons later on.

25

"Brannon," Chris said, taking control of the table again. "I'll give you what you're asking for without hesitation. Whether or not it'll help you, I have no idea, but if it's what you want, you got it. You have to be full in with us though. I don't want you coming along halfheartedly. Do I make myself clear?"

"You give me those written orders, sir, and I'm one hundred percent in just like I always am when we run an op," Brannon assured him.

"Well, that settles that then." Chris smiled and lifted his glass. "I think it's time we got busy saving the world."

The others clinked their glasses to his.

"To Sparta Squad," Caroline said, smiling.

"To being heroes!" Prince beamed.

"To not getting our butts chewed off by demons or something worse," Brannon said, cracking his first smile of the evening.

"Amen," Chris agreed and slugged down the contents of his glass as the others did the same.

****

Breaker Bay 2 was always a bustle of activity around the clock. The mecha kept there were required to be battle ready at all times with two of them actually standing by at alert status for fast deployment. Stealing four super mecha from the bay wasn't going to be easy even for someone with command codes and two Hexers supporting them. The bay was protected by a magic nullifying field technology that kept the Master Travi and Kristen from being able to do anything to help with the theft of the giant machines until they were clear it. That meant Chris and his squad had to get the super mecha outside on their own.

Chris's mech, Chimera Overkill, stood two hundred and fifty-five feet tall. Chimera Overkill was the second largest of the four Spartan mecha. She was equipped with a giant, katana-like blade stored in her back and GAU-19-X Gatling guns mounted on her arms. The Gatling guns were a new design created especially for use by super mecha. They had double the rate of fire as the original GAU-19s and were fed high-velocity, armor-piercing Demon Killer ammo belts mounted in the super mecha's sides. Chimera Overkill also possessed shoulder-mounted rocket launchers containing eight rockets each. She was a war machine of the highest order.

Docked to Chimera Overkill's right was Brannon's massive mecha, Furious Thunder. Furious Thunder stood two hundred and eight feet tall. She was the largest and heaviest of the four super mecha. Furious Thunder was the most heavily armored super mecha still in service. She was designed for close in combat with giant demons. Inside each of her arms were pop out batons that had crushed many demon skulls. They were her primary weapons. However, no super mecha was ever deployed without a ranged combat weapon. As thus, Furious Thunder was also equipped with a giant-sized flamethrower unit concealed within her chest.

Docked to Chimera Overkill's left was Caroline's super mecha, Lightning Dancer. Lightning Dancer was the smallest of the four mecha of Sparta Squad but also in many ways its most dangerous. She was equipped with reactor-powered particle cannons on her wrists, pop-out twin short swords contained on her back, and palm-emplaced missile launchers with a payload of two shots each. Lightning Dancer was the fastest and most agile super mecha ever created.

And docked at the rear of Breaker Bay 2 was Prince's super mecha, Cygnus Rush. On her forearms were mounted massive machine guns identical to Chimera Overkill's. Cygnus Rush also carried the same shoulder-mounted rocket launchers as Chris's mecha. That was where the similarities between the two ended though. Cygnus Rush was a walking mass of firepower. All throughout the super mecha's body were various concealed missile launchers. In total, Cygnus Rush bore seven different launchers with various payloads for each system ranging from guided missiles to even a mini-nuke and two MOABs adapted to function as warheads.

The four super mecha of Spartan Squad were the best of the best that New Busan had in her service in terms of their pilots. Only Reaper Squad rivaled them in firepower and confirmed kills. Reaper Squad was led by Colonel Victor Mal, Chris's longtime nemesis, and stationed in Breaker Bay 4. He and Colonel Mal had completely different approaches to how they led their squads. Chris believed in trust and building relationships while Victor was a big believer in fear and discipline. He had no doubt that if things went badly that General Aketo would task Reaper Squad with stopping them from leaving New Busan. That sort of showdown was the worst thing that could happen. The super mecha of Reaper Squad were equipped with newer weaponry than the super mecha of Spartan Squad and the amount of destruction that would ensue from a conflict between two squads would likely leave entire sections of New Busan in ruins. Chris hoped that Master Travi lived up to his word and got them out of the city without them being forced into such an engagement.

With two of the super mecha of Breaker Bay 2 required to remain on alert at all times, it wasn't hard to get Caroline and Brannon into their machines. They had entered the bay together and headed straight for them, claiming they wanted to run some maintenance on their interface links and targeting systems. Getting himself and Prince into their super mecha had taken a bit more guile.

Chris was the ranking officer of the mecha pilots contained within Breaker Bay 2, only being outranked by the bay's marshal, Higdon. He and Higdon went way back and there was no reason for him to suspect that Chris was up to anything illegal much less as insane as stealing all four of Breaker Bay 2's super mecha in one evening. Chris had requested permission for himself and Prince to enter their super mecha so that they could run the same maintenance that Caroline and Brannon were running. He had made sure the interface link and targeting link checks they were running were ones that were slightly overdue. The request was a bit odd as such checks could be run the bay's tech personnel, but Chris explained that he wanted to do it hands on given the heavier attacks on New Busan's defensive GRIDS. In the end, Marshal Higdon had reluctantly agreed to the small breach in proper procedure given the increased presence and aggressiveness of the demons around the city.

Settling into Chimera Overkill's pilot compartment, Chris jacked into the super mecha's systems. A surge of energy rushed through him as the connection was made. Chris smiled as he began to bring Chimera Overkill's systems online, one by one. He took his time in bringing them up to make things seem as routine as possible and even activated the maintenance programs he had told Marshal Higdon that he would be running. Looking at the tactical display generated by his interface, Chris saw that Brannon and Caroline already had their super mecha fully online. He finished bringing Chimera Overkill fully online as he saw Cygnus Rush appear as a green icon on his display, signaling that Prince was ready now too.

Chris took a deep breath and steeled his nerves for the Hell that was about to break loose in Breaker Bay 2. "Everybody ready?" he asked over the comm-link the four pilots shared. It wasn't their standard combat link through their mecha's systems. Instead, each of them carried a small comm device tuned to an unused, scrambled frequency that only the four of them and the two Hexers, concealed and waiting outside Breaker Bay 2 had access to. Getting the Hexers to take and use the links had been an ordeal in and of itself. Master Travi hated most advanced tech as much as Chris despised magic. Ultimately, the master Hexer had agreed to use them though as there was no other easily feasible means of the group communicating given the anti-magic field in place around the bay.

"All systems go, sir," Brannon confirmed. "We're ready when you are."

"Okay then," Chris said. "Let's get this over with."

Marshal Higdon's voice rang out over Chimera Overkill's comm.

"Colonel," the marshal said. "We're getting some odd readings up here in the control room. Did you just have your entire squad bring their mecha fully online?"

"I did," Chris answered honestly, seeing no point in lying about his intentions anymore. His course was set.

"I didn't authorize you doing that," Marshal Higdon challenged him.

"I am aware of that, Marshal." Chris couldn't help but grin at the confusion in Higdon's voice. "I'm afraid we'll be leaving now too."

"Leaving?" Marshal Higdon rasped. "What in the devil do you mean by that?"

"Sir!" Chris heard a tech in the control with the marshal shouting over the comm behind the sound of Higdon's voice. "The super mecha are. . ."

Chris watched as Furious Thunder began to move. As one of the alert status super mecha in Breaker Bay 2, its path to the exit doors of the bay was already cleared. Furious Thunder's footfall shook the bay as the massive super mecha approached the closed doors and wedged its fingers into the space where they met. Metal whined and bent as Furious Thunder bent the doors inside their frame, pushing them apart. Lightning Dancer was on the move as well. Caroline piloted her with expert grace as the super mecha raced through the opening Furious Thunder had made and outside of the bay.

"Exactly what do you think you're doing?" Marshal Higdon raged at Chris over the comm. "Those super mechas are the property of the New Busan defense force, not your personal toys!"

"Like I said, Marshal," Chris reminded him, "we're leaving and we're going to do what General Aketo refuses to. We're going to end the war with the demons once and for all."

Panicked personnel were attempting to flee Breaker Bay 2 as Chris got Chimera Overkill moving. The super mecha's heavy metal feet clanged against the metal floor of the bay as Chimera Overkill walked towards the torn open exit doors. Furious Thunder as still beside them, watching over the lesser mecha contained in the bay in case any of their alert status pilots got any ideas that might need to be dealt with. Chris prayed that they didn't. The line-unit mechas were no match for the giant powerhouses that Spartan Squad piloted. If they did, an engagement between them would result in a massacre and leave Chris with blood on his hands.

Chimera Overkill and Cygnus Rush reached the exit doors at the same time. Chris held Chimera Overkill back to allow Cygnus Rush to leave the bay first and join Lightning Dancer outside.

"Colonel … Chris," Marshal Higdon pleaded, "I am begging you not to do this. You're throwing away your career!"

"Marshal, I don't see as how I have any other choice," Chris answered.

"If you don't stop, you know we'll be forced to engage you!" Marshal Higdon shouted.

"Unless you have some forces on hand at your disposal I don't know about, I would strongly advise against that, sir," Chris warned.

"Damn you, Chris!" Marshal Higdon raged.

Furious Thunder ducked its massive shoulders and stepped through the bent exit doors of the bay as Chris kept Chimera Overkill in place a bit longer taking one last look at the place that had been his home away from home since the demon plague had spread into Ki-land.

"I'm sorry, Marshal," Chris said sincerely. "I really am, but there is no other way."

"Chris," Higdon's said, his voice sounding sad and filled with regret. "I've ordered Colonel Mal to intercept you. This is your final chance to stand down before he and his squad come at you guns blazing."

"With any luck, Marshal," Chris told him, "we'll be gone before they get here."

Chris estimated that he and his squad had close to three minutes before Reaper Squad's alert status super mecha could be deployed and reach them from Breaker Bay 4. He hoped it would be enough. Switching over to his personal comm link, he tried to contact the two Hexers.

"Master Travi," Chris called over the link, "we're clear of the bay and in position!"

Breaker Bay 2, like all the mecha bays of New Busan, was surrounded by a large open space to give its mecha clear area in which to assemble and await pick up by the transports that usually carried them to whatever combat zone they were needed in. There were no transports in route this time though. If anything, it would be scrambled intercept fighters that were racing towards them where they stood.

A small flash of light appeared on Chris's tactical display as the two Hexers who had been waiting atop a nearby hill stepped out of a dimensional rift onto the open tarmac.

"Colonel Avalon," Master Travi answered him at last and Chris breathed a sigh of relief as he heard the Hexer's voice over his comm. "Prepare yourselves!"

Chris zoomed in on the sight of the two Hexers with Chimera Overkill's augmented visual interface, using the mecha's sensors as his own eyes. Master Travi and his apprentice, Kristen, were waving their hands through the air in strange and elaborate patterns. As their movements built to a crescendo, Master Travi shoved his hands together in a forward motion at the sky in front of where the four super mecha waited. The very air itself shimmered, erupting in flames, as it split apart and a doorway large enough for all four of the super mecha opened.

"Into the breach!" Chris heard Prince shout with unchecked glee and Cygnus Rush dove into the magical portal. The portal flashed brighter as the super mecha made contact with it and then Cygnus Rush was simply gone. Caroline took Lightning Dancer through the portal next.

Chris had no idea where the portal led to. Master Travi hadn't taken the time to inform him of their initial destination and Chris didn't really care. As long it wasn't here, it was good enough for now.

"You should go next, sir," Brannon said as Furious Thunder took up a defensive position next to the portal. "We've got boogies inbound!"

Chris swiveled around Chimera Overkill's tactical view to see two super mecha approaching them from the north. One stood roughly three hundred feet tall, all black and glimmering armor, a gigantic battle axe clutched in its hands. Chris recognized it as Colonel Mal's personal mecha, Midnight Blighter. Slightly behind it came another super mecha, Skull Tank. Skull Tank wasn't as large as Midnight Blighter but what it lacked in height it more than made up for in bulk. Instead of legs, Skull Tank rode along the ground on twin tank-like treads. Skull Tank had no proper head; instead, a snarling skeletal face was centered in the middle of its chest. Its two eyes glowed, powering up, to deliver a blast of energy at Chimera Overkill that was going to hurt like hell if it made contact.

"Go Brannon!" Chris ordered his second-in-command as locked onto Skull Tank's snarling face with his shoulder rocket launchers. Thankfully, Brannon obeyed his orders and Furious Thunder's massive form entered the shimmering portal the Hexers had conjured up.

Chris found himself unable to make a preemptive strike against the oncoming super mecha. No matter how much he disliked Colonel Mal and his Reapers, they still fought for the same thing: the safety of New Busan. The two Reapers apparently didn't feel how he did though. Skull Tank's eyes flashed as they took their shot at Chimera Overkill. Chris braced himself against the impact of the blast as it struck Chimera Overkill, nearly severing the super mecha's right arm at its shoulder joint and slagging the armor there. Chris knew better than to try to reason with Colonel Mal so he wasted no time in making the attempt. Slamming Chimera Overkill's servo-motors into overdrive, he whirled the super mecha about. Chimera Overkill leaped for the portal and vanished through it as a blinding flash of light swept over the two Reaper Squad super mecha and the entire area outside of Breaker Bay 2.

****

Chris experienced a sensation akin to falling as Chimera Overkill toppled through the interdimensional void the portal had opened into. It ended abruptly as the two hundred and fifty foot tall super mecha came tumbling out of the portal to go rolling across the sands of a vast desert. The impact almost ripped Chimera Overkill's badly damaged right arm away from the super mecha's body. When Chimera Overkill finally came to a stop, Chris took a moment to collect himself before he brought Chimera Overkill back onto its feet. As the super mecha stood up to its full height, Chris noticed that the other three super mecha of Spartan Squad were standing motionless, their pilots awaiting his orders. The portal was no more. It had closed as Chimera Overkill passed through it.

"Glad to see you could join us, sir," Caroline's voice came over his personal comm. He figured she must be using her personal comm rather than her super mecha's so that the two Hexers who stood at the feet of the four giants could hear what was being said too.

"Looks like you took a pretty bad hit, sir," Brannon commented.

"Nothing I could do about that," Chris lied, knowing full well that he could have shot Skull Tank before the Reaper mecha fired at him. "It is what it is."

"What it is, is pretty serious," Prince chimed in. "Ain't no repair bays out here in the Wastelands."

"The Wastelands?" Chris asked. "Is that where we are?"

Chris took another look around at the ominous, dark skies above the sea of sand Chimera Overkill and the others stood in. Distant lightning flared among the black clouds that bloated out the sun.

"The Wastelands were the safest place I could think of to port four super mecha to, Colonel Avalon," Master Travi's voice crackled over his comm. "Plenty of space out here to regroup and figure out where we're going next, and the demons shy away from this place as much as we humans do."

"Makes sense," Chris agreed. "But why didn't you just take us straight to America? Surely there was somewhere closer to the Nexus we could have ported to."

"I am a master Hexer, Colonel Avalon, not a god," Master Travi told him. "Transporting four super mecha is not an easy feat. You and your squad are blessed that we didn't lose one of you in the transition."

"Just helping conjure that portal cost me a year of my life, Colonel Avalon," Kristen informed him. "All magic comes with a price."

Chris frowned as the Hexer's words fully hit him. "I had no idea it would be so rough on the two of you," he said in way of an apology.

"I'm young, Colonel," Kristen replied, laughing, "I have years to spare, and if giving up a few in order to save all of Ki-land is the price to be paid, then I do it gladly. We have several more such transports to make before we reach the Nexus."

"What do you mean several more?" Chris asked.

"I promised I would see you to the Nexus, Colonel Avalon," Master Travi said, "but I cannot take you directly there. The corruption that the demons have brought to Ki-land has skewed the paths we Hexers use when making our conjurations. We will require a minimum of two more such jumps as this one to reach the shores of America and then the Nexus."

"Colonel," Brannon cut in. "We're going to need to do something about that arm, sir. There's no point in making it to the Nexus if we aren't battle ready when we reach it."

"I promised you passage not safe passage," Master Travi snorted. "However, I can mend the damaged arm of your super mecha if you so desire."

"You can?" Prince blurted out before Chris could reply.

"We will need time to recover before we can conjure another portal in any case," Master Travi said. "Doing so will add to that time, but mending your suit is not outside of my power to do."

"How much time are we talking?" Brannon asked as Chris already began to think over the offer.

"Enough time to rest and recharge," Master Travi answered. "Eight hours, perhaps ten."

"Done," Chris said, agreeing to Master Travi's offer.

"We sleeping in our suits then, sir?" Caroline asked.

"No bloody way!" Prince laughed. "I've never been outside of New Busan before. I bet you guys haven't either. This is our chance to see the world with our own bodies, not through our suits' sensors."

"Three off, one on," Chris ordered. "Brannon, you mind taking first watch?"

"My pleasure, Colonel," Brannon answered. "This place gives me the creeps. I'd feel a lot better keeping eighteen hundred tons of metal around me."

Chris, Caroline, and Prince left their super mecha to join the two Hexers on the ground below. All mecha pilots were required to take a course on survival should their suit be damaged beyond functionality behind enemy lines. Given how barren the Wastelands were, it took some time to scrap together enough flammable material from the scattered, rotting foliage to make a fire, but they managed it. Each of the super mechas had its own survival gear stored in a crammed-full backpack that was kept in the pilot's compartment for easy emergency access. For the time being, food and water weren't going to be an issue as he each pack of survival gear contained enough, when rationed, to last a normal person for three days.

The two Hexers had brought nothing with them and were far too drained and exhausted to conjure up anything for their needs, so Chris and his squad had to share. Chris handed Master Travi a bottle of water which the master Hexer accepted gratefully. Prince's excitement at being in the Wastelands kept him from resting so he relinquished his sleeping bag to Kristen. The younger Hexer was stretched out and asleep beside the crackling, small fire of the group's makeshift camp within a matter of minutes.

Chris and the others shared a quick meal of combat rations and water as they sat around the fire. Lightning continued to flash and dance among the dark clouds as night in the Wastelands truly fell. No thunder accompanied the flashes of energy in the sky, and Chris had begun to accept them as the natural state of the blighted place. The flashes seemed mystical in origin, but he couldn't bring himself to ask Master Travi about them. He wasn't entirely sure he wanted to know the answer as to what and why they were. Master

Travi was on the verge of collapse at any rate and Chris knew it was better to let the Hexer rest. The master Hexer didn't ask for a sleeping bag though; instead, he simply crossed his legs upon the sand where he sat and closed his eyes entering a trance-like state resembling the one he had been in when Chris had first met him. Chris supposed it was a form a mystical meditation that the master Hexer preferred in situations like this over true sleep.

"Check this thing out!" Prince called as he came back to the fire after vanishing to go exploring the area around the camp. He carried a creature the size of a clenched fist impaled upon the end of a stick. The creature had four cat-like legs attached to the body of a scorpion and a head bristling with antenna. "I mean, what in the heck is it?"

"Whatever it is, keep it away from me," Chris warned him.

"Did you really have to kill it, Prince?" Caroline asked as she stared at the creature's limp body where it dangled from the point of the stick he held it on.

"I am pretty sure it tried to kill me first," Prince said, frowning at her.

"He's likely right about that too," Chris commented. "If I remember the briefing we got about this place correctly, everything out here is hostile and deadly."

"I will be glad when this night is over with." Caroline hugged her arms about her body as if she were cold. She couldn't be though. The temperature had risen with the falling of true night in the Wastelands, not dropped.

Chris was sweating as chugged down the last of his bottled water. He wiped at his brow to keep it from dripping into his eyes.

"You know," Prince grinned, "this place is a lot like what you think Hell would be like."

Chris couldn't argue with him so he simply nodded. "Look, let's just get some rest like our Hexer friends are doing. Tomorrow's a new day, and I expect it will be a lot rougher of one too."

****

There was no true sunrise in the Wastelands, though eventually a few, weak rays of light did pierce the dense dark clouds above the group's makeshift camp as they came awake and began to prepare for the day ahead. Chris had taken time during the night to use his Player Character ability of scanning the two Hexers. He was astounded to have found that Master Travi was a level twenty-two Hexer. Such a level was rare among NPCs. Most NPCs never topped twenty. Master Travi's level certainly explained how the man had transported four super mechas without the aid of a talisman or magical artifact. Kristen, it turned out, was a level fourteen Hexer. Her level was at least what he had expected to see upon taking a closer look at her. Her stats though … Master Travi had not been exaggerating about her potential. Kristen's magical aptitude rank was well above what it should be for a level fourteen Hexer. She appeared to be on the edge of leveling up too. Chris knew that it would happen sooner rather than later with the demands that his quest for the Nexus would put upon her.

Chris had also managed to get a look at things back home via his interface with Ki, the game's A.I. General Aketo was just as furious as Chris had expected him to be. Colonel Mal was just as ticked off at his and the rest of Sparta Squad's escape from New Busan. Mal was chomping at the bit for General Aketo to allow him to take Reaper Squad out of the city in pursuit of them. Thankfully, as yet, the general was refusing to allow Colonel Mal to do so. New Busan's defense was more important to the general than even four of the city's super mecha being stolen. There was no question that General Aketo knew exactly where he and his Spartans were headed for. Maybe the general hoped that they would succeed on some level despite the bitterness at the betrayal Chris stung him with.

"Good morning, Colonel Avalon." Master Travi smiled at him, looking like a new man. Clearly, the master Hexer had gotten the rest he had needed.

"Morning, Master Travi," Chris replied, nodding at him. Both Caroline and Prince had returned to their super mecha during the course of the night as their watches had come up. Brannon had never left pilot compartment of Furious Thunder, but Chris hoped his second-in-command had gotten some sleep regardless. He'd spent many a night himself in Chimera Overkill's and knew that it was possible.

"Now, shall we see about attending that super mecha of yours?" Master Travi asked.

"Any time you feel up to it," Chris answered.

Master Travi nodded. "I shall be about it then."

"Kristen!" Master Travi called. "If you would join me, please."

"Of course, Master." The young Hexer was back in full stride as well though she did appear a hair breath older than the day before. Chris could see that Kristen had been telling the truth when she had claimed that helping her master with the conjuring of the portal had cost her a year of her mortal life.

Together, the two Hexers concentrated their power on Chimera Overkill. Their chant was a brief one with much fewer arcane gestures than the massive portal had required. The damaged arm of Chris's super mecha glowed, surrounded by an aura of orange light, as its metal was reshaped and the damage it had taken erased from the reality of the game.

Chris heard a voice inside his head say, "Eighteen Mega points restored!"

The statement was instantly followed by quieter one that said, "Hexer, Kristen Peek, new level achieved."

Banishing the voice of Ki-land's controlling A.I. from his head, Chris stared in awe at Chimera Overkill. The super mecha's right arm looked as flawless and fully functional as it had before the Reaper Squad super mecha, Skull Tank, had blasted it.

"Thank you," Chris stammered when he was finally able to tear his gaze away from his repaired super mecha.

"It benefits us all, Colonel, to have you at your strongest." Master Travi half-bowed. "Return to your suit and we shall begin our travels for the day."

Chris entered Chimera Overkill and was transported by the suit's systems to his pilot compartment. Chimera Overkill's control lit up as he strapped in and linked up to the super mecha. His tactical display sprang to life before his eyes filling his field of vision. All of the giant suit's systems were online and green, ready for action.

"Okay, Master Travi," Chris said over the comm. link shared by the entire group. "It's your show. Take us to where we need to go."

The two Hexers once again expended the bulk of their power to open a gleaming portal that shined like a sun in the darkness of the Wastelands.

"Take heed, Colonel, that this time, I cannot promise you safety once you arrive on the other side," Master Travi cautioned him as Chris got Chimera Overkill moving towards the portal.

"Understood," he answered. "I've got point. Brannon, I want you through right after me, weapons at the ready."

"Yes, sir. I'll be right behind you," Chris heard Brannon answer before Chimera Overkill entered the portal.

Chimera Overkill stepped out of the portal's other side and into a war zone. The super mecha found itself on the streets of a once great city Chris recognized as Chicago. The ruins of skyscrapers surrounded it, some of them burning. Spirals of thick, curling smoke rose towards the heavens. American jet fighters streaked through the air, launching salvos of missiles at horrid, monstrous beasts that filled the air with high-pitched battle cries. The creatures sped, carried by leathery, black wings, dodging the Americans' fire and then swooped in to directly engage the jet fighters. Chris watched as one of the creatures rammed one of the jet fighters head on. It tore through the jet and flew onward through its exploding remains. Tracer rounds flashed as another jet fell in behind the creature and opened fire on it with its forward cannons. The creature shrieked as the rounds peppered its back with gaping holes and shredded its wings.

New Busan had lost contact with the city state of Chicago a week previous and it was easy to see why. The demons had broken through the city's defenses and now rampaged through it, killing every living thing they came across. The city had been one of the last holdouts of humanity in the States. Chris was amazed that there was any resistance left to stand against the hordes of demons but somehow, someone was hanging on and putting up a fight. The jet fighters had to have launched from somewhere within the city and that meant there had to be centralized strong point somewhere within it.

Chris was torn from his thoughts as one of the winged creatures set its sights on Chimera Overkill and came flying towards the super mecha. Chimera Overkill raised one of her hands, the Gatling gun mounted on her arm hosing the incoming monster with so many rounds that it disintegrated in an explosion of pulped flesh and vile, black blood. The blast drew the attention of the other demon flyers. Several more of the creatures disengaged from their battle with the American jet fighters, their attention now fixated on the new, larger threat to their existence.

Furious Thunder emerged from the portal behind Chimera Overkill. Her arm batons were out and ready. Seeing the mass of creatures approaching Chimera Overkill, Brannon already had her moving to intercept them. Chris knew that Brannon could handle the monsters so he gave him no order to stop. Furious Thunder stepped into the flight path of the inbound creatures and met them with a barrage of blows that crushed bones and shattered bodies, knocking most of them from the air within seconds.

Cygnus Rush came through the portal next, and seeing what was taking place, Prince positioned her into a firing position well behind the other two super mecha.

"Prince!" Chris yelled over the comm. "Can you clear the air?"

"On it, boss!" Prince answered him.

Two seconds later, dozens of missiles flew from Cygnus Rush, each of them targeting one of the winged, demon creatures. Fiery blasts rippled across the sky above the city of Chicago as the demon things died one after another.

Chimera Overkill's systems informed Chris that one of the American jet fighters was trying to hail him. He switched over to the comm frequency the fighters were using.

"Whoever you are, thanks for the assist!" a female voice with a deep southern accent shouted.

Lightning Dancer had made it through the portal now too and the dimensional gateway had collapsed upon itself. Chris knew that Master Travi and Kristen had to have come through as well, but he couldn't see any sign of them.

"This is Colonel Avalon of the New Busan defense force," Chris responded to the American pilot. "Glad we could help out. Just how bad are things here?"

"New Busan?" he heard the female pilot gasp. "That's a heck of a long way from here. What in the devil are you doing in our city?"

"Passing through," Chris answered.

When he said nothing more, the female pilot answered his question. "How bad is it here? Take a look around, Colonel. Chicago is burning. The demons overran our defenses. All our mecha and supers are gone. The city has fallen. We're down to one combat effective base on the city's southern edge and it's flooded with refugees fleeing the demons."

Chris raised an eyebrow at the pilot's mention of supers. He had forgotten that in the states, such things existed. There were no supers in New Busan. Supers were ordinary people who with the coming of the demon plague suddenly manifested powers and abilities far beyond the scope of normal humanity. Some of them reportedly possessed super speed and could run faster than the speed of sound, others could tear through steel with their bare hands, and others still could do even more bizarre things such as shoot flames from their hands or energy blasts from their eyes. According to what little he remembered about them, supers, unlike Hexers and most Psionicists, had chosen to enter the war with the demons full on and served side by side with America's human defenders.

"I suggest you get clear of the heart of the city, Colonel," the female pilot warned him. "There's not really anywhere here to hide those super mechas of yours and you're about to be the target of every demon close enough around to realize that you guys are here!"

"Understood," Chris acknowledged. "And thanks for the heads up."

The surviving jet fighters headed south, leaving the four super mecha standing amid the destruction the demons had wrought upon the city of Chicago. There were hundreds of human-sized demons in the streets around the super mecha. They were howling and attacking their feet. Claws sparked as they raked against the armor of the super mecha. A few of the braver demons even began to attempt to climb up their feet and legs.

"Uh, boss," Prince chimed in. "I am pretty sure these little guys can't hurt us but …"

"I know." Chris nodded though he knew Prince couldn't see him. "Let's get moving and try to find somewhere safer to be."

"What about Master Travi and Kristen?" Caroline asked.

"I'm sure they can take care of themselves," Chris told her. "For all we know, they're already out of this madness and waiting on us to catch up to them. We'll try to make contact with them while we're on the move."

The four super mecha moved out. Demons fell from the armor of their feet and legs while others scrambled out their path. Not all of the fleeing demons were able to escape their footfalls though. The street was stained black with the blood of those who weren't able to.

"Picking up something big ahead, sir," Brannon called out over the unit's comm-link.

Two skyscrapers ahead of the mecha came tumbling down in a shower of shattering glass and toppling debris as a demon even larger than Furious Thunder crashed through them. Its yellow eyes blazed with hellish hatred as it saw the metal giants. The thing moved on two legs like a person. Its body was thin and sleek though its arms were thick and rippled with muscles. It gave the impression of a lizard boxer crossed with an ape. Gray, armor-like scales covered its entire body from head to toe. A forked tongue flicked from its mouth every so often as if it were using it to sniff the air like a snake. Its tail stretched into the distance behind it as it barreled towards the closest of the super mecha.

Furious Thunder barely had time counter the first of the demon's blow. A clenched fist came at the mecha's head. One of Furious Thunder's batons caught the underside of the demon's arm at the last moment, knocking it off its intended course. Furious Thunder blocked a second blow from the beast that struck with such force that it might have torn the super mecha in two had it hit unchecked.

As Furious Thunder staggered away from the beast, Caroline moved Lightning Dancer in. Lightning Dancer's twin short swords were out. The smaller super mecha moved with a speed that seemed impossible for the giant demon to match. Her blades slashed deep grooves through the flesh of the beast's upper legs and thighs. The demon beast roared in anger as it launched itself at her and missed plowing into and toppling another building. Lightning Dancer didn't let up her attack. As the demon beast tried to recover, her swords sliced along the length of its back as its blood spurted over her. The demon beast's blood boiled and smoked where it made contact with Lightning Dancer.

The blood is acid based, KI, the game's A.I., informed Chris inside his mind.

"Get out of there, Caroline!" Chris ordered Lightning Dancer. "You can't stop that thing alone!"

Lightning Dancer whirled about, dashing away from the demon beast as holes formed in her armor where the thing's blood ate away at it.

Chimera Overkill's sword shot upwards out of its back as the armor there opened and the resealed itself. The super mecha caught the hilt of the sword with an uncanny grace, bringing it up into a defensive hold.

"Hey, ugly!" Chris called at the demon beast through Chimera Overkill's external speakers, his voice amplified to thunderous proportions.

The demon beast glared at Chimera Overkill and reared its back in a new roar of anger and challenge. It came charging at Chimera Overkill, hissing as its forked tongue whipped out of its mouth. Chris made no attempt at dodging the monster until the last possible moment. As the demon beast reached Chimera Overkill, the super mecha swung its katana-like blade, stepping just enough to the right to avoid the monster ramming into it. The demon beast stumbled forward, black blood pouring from where its left arm had been attached to its shoulder. As the creature began to feel the pain of its missing arm, it shrieked like a banshee. Windows blew out in the buildings closest to where it stood, raining shards of glass onto the street below.

Chris allowed himself a smile. It was quickly wiped from his face though as the demon beast's tail wrapped around Chimera Overkill's left leg and with a jerk, brought the super mecha crashing down. Pavement broke beneath Chimera Overkill as Chris was jarred about inside its pilot's compartment. Only the straps of his safety harness kept the damage he took from being worse. As it was, he was merely bruised and shaken up.

"Colonel!" he heard Brannon yelling over his comm-link.

Furious Thunder ran at the demon beast, tackling it like a football player. The two of them went tumbling along the streets of Chicago, leaving a trail of carnage in their wake as they rolled over the masses of human-sized demons that infested them. Their rolling ended with Furious Thunder on top. One of the super mecha's giant hands plunged down the demon beast's throat, breaking its jaws and tearing its throat apart in the process. The demon beast's body spasmed and twitched beneath the weight of Furious Thunder as the beast shook in its death throes.

RESPAWNING … RESPAWNING … RESPAWNING … a voice from out of nowhere boomed.

"What the …?" Chris muttered, shocked, as he got Chimera Overkill back onto her feet. Nothing in Ki-land was supposed to respawn. That wasn't how things worked in the game. Nonetheless, it appeared to be happening.

"What was that?" Caroline shouted over the comm-link.

"I thought that crap only happened in video games!" Prince protested the reality of the situation.

The body of the demon beast vanished from beneath Furious Thunder and reappeared, completely whole and new behind where Chimera Overkill stood.

"Oh crap," Chris had time to say before the demon beast's tail whipped through the air and slammed into Chimera Overkill's right side. Armor crunched as the massive super mecha was hurled into a skyscraper by the force of the tail's blow.

"Don't worry, Colonel, I got this mother!" Prince shouted.

"No!" Chris ordered. "Save your missiles. We're going to need them!"

Furious Thunder sprinted at the demon beast, but this time, it was ready. It met each of the super mecha's baton strikes with the upper sides of its arms, blocking each blow as they swung towards it. Brannon outsmarted the monster though. He feinted and then delivered a baton below to its side that knocked the breath from the demon beast's lungs. It staggered backwards as Lightning Dancer came leaping around Furious Thunder to engage the demon beast, her blades a blur of motion as they slashed through the monster's flesh time and time again. The damage Lightning Dancer had taken earlier from the demon beast's blood appeared mostly cosmetic in nature and she struck at the thing in relentless frenzy.

"Out of the way!" Prince screamed at the two of them. Furious Thunder stumbled sideways as Lightning Dancer sped off in the opposite direction.

"Don't!" Chris ordered Prince again.

"Sorry, sir, just one!" Prince laughed as Cygnus Rush raised a single, open palm up in at the demon beast. The cover of the missile tube embedded in the super mecha's arm dilated open. A fraction of a second later, a single projectile shot from Cygnus Rush's palm. It slammed into the demon beast's forehead, wedging itself into the bone there and then exploded. The demon beast's head blew apart in a shower of gore and bone fragments. Its headless body gave a single twitch and then collapsed to the ground.

"Nice shot," Caroline commented as Cygnus Rush slowly lowered its raised arm.

"Thanks." Prince chuckled and then added before Chris could speak up, "It was only one missile, sir. Didn't have the time to tell you what I was planning. Sorry about that."

"You got the job done," Chris grunted. "That's what matters, but don't make a habit of this or I'll have you up on charges, assuming we survive to make this field trip and make it home.

Now, we really need to get out of here before any more of those things show up."

"What was that voice, sir?" Caroline asked. "The one that sounded like something out of a video game?"

"No idea," Chris lied. "It doesn't matter. Like I said, what matters is that we keep moving."

"Yes, sir," Caroline replied, but Chris could tell she wasn't happy with his answer.

Chris had no idea where they should even head for. He didn't want to try for Chicago's last defense base. Whoever was in charge there would have far too many questions that he didn't have the time to answer. He didn't want to get sucked into the battle that was raging throughout the city any more than they already had either. There still had been no contact from the two Hexers. Chris could only hope they were okay because if they weren't, he and the rest of Spartan Squad were utterly fragged.

Activating his personal comm-link, he tried to raise the two Hexers. "Master Travi, this is Colonel Avalon. Do you read me?"

"I hear you, Colonel," Master Travi's voice responded almost instantly.

"Where in the holy Hades are you two?" Chris demanded.

"The streets were rather … crowded when we emerged from the portal, Colonel. Drained from our transit, our only choice was to flee. We used the last of our energy to teleport ourselves to the top of a building on the city's eastside. I am afraid I am unable to tell you its precise location," Master Travi informed him. "Thankfully, we do appear safe at least for the time being here. There has been no sign of the demons within the building as yet."

"Don't worry about giving me your location. Just stay where you are. We can use the comm-link's signal to locate you," Chris told him. "We need to meet up and get out of this city as fast as possible."

"Colonel," Master Travi spoke with a deep sadness in his voice, "you are aware that we will not be able to open such a portal again until we have rested."

"It will take us some time to lock onto your signal and find you. Just how long do you need minimum?" Chris asked.

"Perhaps more time than you can grant us, Colonel," Master Travi said. "Four hours at best, and even then, opening another such portal will be risky."

"Understood," Chris answered. "We're on our way to get you. We'll figure the rest out when we arrive."

Chris switched over to Chimera Overkill's combat link. "I've made contact with Master Travi and Kristen. They're okay for the time being. We need to get to them through as fast as we can. I'll be tracing the signal of their comm-link to find them so form up on me and follow my lead."

The signal from the two Hexers' comm-links was coming from the west. Chris was impressed at how far the two surely exhausted spell slingers had managed to teleport themselves to escape the demons they had encountered. The extra strain it must have put on them had to be staggering too.

Chimera Overkill stomped through the streets of Chicago, heading westward, with Furious Thunder following on her heels. Lightning Dancer and Cygnus Rush brought up the rear, trailing a slight distance behind them, keeping the mecha squad spread out enough not be a centralized target for the demons that surely had to be watching them by now. Four super mecha on the move was a difficult thing to miss. The question was whether the demons would engage them again or not before they could reach the two Hexers. The four super mecha were moving at little more than a cautious walking pace, as Chris didn't know what might be waiting on them as they moved through the city. Even so, that put their speed at a solid forty-five miles an hour. He hoped to reach the Hexers in less than twenty minutes. Of course, when you were in a demon infested, nightmarish hell of a city, twenty minutes could be a very long time.

There was a constant stream of hails pinging Chimera Overkill's comm from Chicago's last defense base. Chris made a point not to acknowledge them and ordered the others to do the same. As powerful as they were, four super mechas weren't enough to save the city. They would die in vain if they tried. Their focus had to remain on reaching the Nexus and nothing else.

Not believing what he was seeing up ahead of the four super mechas, Chris brought Chimera Overkill to an abrupt halt nearly, causing Brannon in Furious Thunder to ram into him. Furious Thunder's hand shot up, motioning for Lightning Dancer and Cygnus Rush to come to a stop behind them.

The very street itself was heaving upwards in a long trail that stretched on beyond Chris's line of sight. Something beneath it was rippling the concrete and pavement above it as it moved in the direction of the super mecha.

"What in the devil is that?" Brannon asked, apparently seeing it too.

"Weapons hot!" Chris ordered as the fragments of the street and road in front of the super mecha were hurled skyward as a giant worm with tentacles flailing about it behind its razor-toothed screeching mouth exploded upwards from the city's sewers. The creature's tentacles lashed out to ensnare Chimera Overkill's arms before Chris could manage to open fire with the super mecha's arm-mounted Gatling guns. The tentacles yanked the super mecha towards its open mouth even as Chimera Overkill fought to break their hold on her.

The only thing that saved Chimera Overkill from being demon worm food was Lightning Dancer. The smaller super mecha sprinted between the two of them, severing the tentacles that clutched Chimera Overkill's arms with the blades of her matching short swords. Spurting black blood, the remainder of the tentacles that had held Chimera Overkill jerked away from her as Lightning Dancer moved in closer still to the worm, blades batting away and cutting new tentacles that reached out to grab her.

The body of the demon worm seemed to convulse before a geyser of yellow liquid came spraying from its mouth at Lightning Dancer. Any other super mecha would have been struck by it, but Lightning Dancer was the fastest super mecha ever built. She swerved out of the liquid's path, twisting as she leaped through the air to crash into a nearby building. The side of it she land on shattered behind her wake, bringing the rest of the building down on top of her. Covered in wreckage, she was saved from the worm's deadly spray but also out of the fight for the time being.

The yellow liquid was even more acidic than the blood of the demon creature they had slain earlier. It didn't bubble and smoke on the things it landed on, it melted them into nothingness almost instantaneously.

"Don't let that crap hit you!" Chris called to the others as Chimera Overkill's Gatling guns took aim at the demon worm and began to spin, hosing it with a barrage of high-powered, high-velocity rounds. The bullets ripped gaping holes in the worm's soft flesh, tearing through its body to leave even larger exit wounds. Chris breathed a sigh of relief as the demon worm drew itself up to a height that dwarfed that of Chimera Overkill's and then thudded, unmoving onto the rumble of the streets it had come from.

"Is it dead?" Brannon asked.

"Let's make sure," Prince said. "I suggest y'all find some cover!"

Both Chimera Overkill and Furious Thunder stepped off the street they had been moving along to hunker down behind the closest buildings to them.

A fraction of a second later, two missiles blazed out of Cygnus Rush's shoulder launchers to blow what was left of the worm to bits and pieces.

"I'd say it's dead," Chris commented as Chimera Overkill rose back to her feet. "Somebody help Caroline!"

Though Lightning Dancer was already digging her own way out of the debris of the building that had fallen on her, Furious Thunder gave her a hand to speed up the process.

"How many more of these things are we going to have to kill, boss?" Caroline griped. "I have system errors all over the place in here."

"How bad?" Chris asked, truly concerned as he knew they all had a long way to go.

"Nothing really serious yet," Caroline answered, "but I'm down to eighty-five percent of my normal speed and the servos in my right arm are threatening to lockdown from the damage I've taken."

"We'll do what we can to fix them after we get out of this city," Chris told her. "It could be a lot worse."

"Don't even say that," Caroline grumbled at him.

"Sir, we seriously need to keep moving," Brannon urged.

"Right," Chris agreed as he kicked Chimera Overkill into gear and the super mecha lurched forward, taking the lead again.

****

Chris felt the world imploding around him. It was like reality itself collapsing on him and burying him in a sea of darkness. His hands shot upwards as he screamed. They thudded against the canopy of his game pod. The impact shook the canopy above him as he began to realize where he was. He was back in the real world aboard the Orb. Something had gone wrong. Chris slumped, relaxing somewhat inside the game pod. At least he was alive. For a moment, he had been afraid a giant demon beast had caught him off guard in Chimera Overkill and that the end had come for him at last.

His panic began to return as he came more awake. The power to the game pod was offline. That meant something had happened aboard the Orb. Before he had entered Ki-land, the Orb's power systems had checked out and showed no signs of any problems. It didn't make sense for the station's power to just kick out. He didn't want to damage his game pod, but he needed to get out of it, and without power to it, that was going to take some effort. Rolling in the cramped space of the game pod, he found the manual release for its canopy and went to work removing the small panel that covered its controls. Popping the panel loose, he carefully removed it and reached behind where it had sat to pull the lever that forced the game pod's canopy open. He breathed a sigh of release as the panel responded and rose upwards to release him from the pod.

Chris leaped out of the game pod. The lights weren't completely off in the section of the Orb where the game pods were located. They glowed a dim red, which told him that the station's emergency power had kicked in. There were entire sections of the station that he had personally reduced or cut power to, but this area wasn't one of them. He always kept the station's power fully online in the game area. Entering Ki-land was his only escape from the nightmare that real life had become since the plague. As far as he knew, he was the only living human to have survived the plague that had decimated the Earth below. Ki-land meant everything to him now. It was his life. Chris had no other life left.

The trip to the Orb's bridge was a hurried one. Chris moved as fast as he could through the Z gravity areas of the station using a technique of bouncing off one of the station's surfaces to another using its walls to increase his momentum and speed as he went. He caught himself, bringing his body to a stop, as he reached the doors to the station's bridge. Lowering himself to them, he watched as they opened in front him, thankful that they too still had power despite whatever was going in the game area of the station. Chris flopped onto the bridge and raced to his seat at its control console, strapping himself into it. His fingers flew over the keys there as he brought up a readout on the Orb's systems. He saw at a glance that there were error codes everywhere throughout the station. A quick check told him that the Orb's shields and thrusters were still online. He ran a check with the station's sensors next. His breath caught in his chest as watched the data they gave him pouring across the screen of the console. A satellite had intercepted the Orb's path while he was inside the game and had been smashed apart against the station's shields. They had mostly done their job of protecting the station from the impact of the debris, but it appeared at least one smaller piece of the satellite had gotten through the shields. It had struck dangerously close to the Orb's main reactor core. From the readings he was getting, the damage didn't look too bad. It was just enough to cause a disruption in the Orb's overall power distribution, not knock it offline. Chris frowned as he saw that he was going to have to make the repairs that needed to be made manually. Time stopped for his character in Ki-land when he was outside of the game, but not for the entire game world. He didn't understand the mechanics of how that worked exactly, but he knew it to be true. When he re-entered Ki-land, he would do so at the exact time and place where he had been forced out due to the power loss in the Orb, but the infection and disruptions to the game's core programming would continue as they were in real time with him. He needed to get back into Ki-land as fast as possible. Though he was just one man and couldn't save the world he had grown up in, Chris truly believed he could save Ki-land from the same fate that the Earth had suffered.

Pausing only long enough to grab the box of tools he kept on the station's bridge, Chris rushed out into the Orb's winding system of corridors once more. He took the shortest path he could towards where the bit of destroyed satellite had struck the station. Bouncing from one wall to the next in the Orb's zero G atmosphere, he made it there in just a matter of minutes. As the doors to the section of engineering where the impact had occurred opened, his eyes bugged. There was a metal shard, slightly larger than his arm, impaling the wall of the Orb. As it entered, it must have cut through a power conduit or at least that was all he could figure. The angle the metal shard entered at had made it where the shard sealed itself in the wall avoiding decompression in the area. Nonetheless, he sprayed the entire area where the metal shard was with a foam sealant to ensure that a sudden decompression wouldn't take him by surprise as he worked on getting the Orb's power fixed. It needed to be done anyway. If the shard shifted in the slightest, there would have been a true hole that opened into space and whole other kinds of problems to deal with.

Bypassing the section of power conduit the piece of satellite had severed went smoothly. The process took less than half an hour even with him working alone. Chris was fully aware of just how blessed he had been. Had the piece of satellite impacted the station differently, he might be dead right now. With the work completed, he raced back to the bridge to double check that the station was out of danger and that its power levels throughout had returned to the settings he had established for them. He triple checked the Orb's shields making sure they were fully functional and operating as they were designed to. Chris paused, looking at the Orb's communications console. A part of him wanted to try to reach someone, anyone to tell them about what had happened and how he had just saved himself and the Orb from a situation that could have easily escalated into something deadly. It took a great deal of willpower, but he turned his eyes away from the communications console. Rationally, he knew that there was no one out there to answer him no matter how more time he invested in trying. Ki-land was waiting for him and he needed desperately to get back into the game.

Chris's stomach grumbled, reminding him of just how long he had been in the game before the incident with the satellite had forced him out of it. He stopped by the station's mess to wolf down some cereal and chug a bottle of water before he started for the Orb's game section. The whole mess had left him rather shaken up. Ki-land was depending on him to save it. He was the only one who could. Or at least that's what he told himself to stay sane.

He returned to his game pod and finally began to relax as its canopy cover closed over him. Chris closed his eyes and allowed his consciousness to be sucked into the world of Ki-land. Then he was inside of Chimera Overkill again as the super mecha walked through the war-torn streets of Chicago.

****

"Colonel?" Chris heard Brannon calling to him over Chimera Overkill's comm. "Colonel, are you there?"

"I'm here," Chris answered. "I was just taking a moment to get my head together."

The situation in the game world hadn't changed just as Chris knew it wouldn't have. He and the rest of Spartan Squad were still homing in on the comm signal from the two Hexers with their four super mecha in route to the spell slingers' position.

"Colonel, I'm picking up more of those winged demons approaching from the south," Prince informed him.

Chris checked Prince's data with Chimera Overkill's own sensors. There were a few dozen of the monsters, but they didn't seem to be on a direct flight path towards the super mecha. They could be heading for anywhere in the city.

"I see them," Chris responded. "It doesn't look like they are coming at us though. Until they shift their course and we know that they are, I think it's a good idea to leave them alone. No sense in bringing more trouble down on us if we don't have to."

"Yes, sir," Prince replied accepting his decision.

"Estimated time to the Hexers' position?" Chris asked.

"Less than three minutes, sir," Brannon chimed in. "We've covered a lot of ground already."

"I think it's time we picked up our pace then before those winged demons do decide they want to try to get a piece of us," Chris ordered.

The four super mecha double timed it towards the distant building where the two Hexers were waiting. Chris knew Prince would be keeping a close eye on the winged demons so he entrusted that job to him and kept his focus on what lay ahead of them. Even when they reached the two Hexers, there would be no quick escape from the city of Chicago. Master Travi and Kristen were going to need more time to recover before the two of them could open another portal large enough for the super mecha to transit out of the city through. Chris hoped Master Travi had come up with a plan, but right now, he sure didn't have one besides standing around and waiting. And that was just asking for the demons in the city to get organized and make a real, full-on run at them.

"Colonel Avalon," Master Travi's voice came over his personal comm-link. "We have visual on your squad. I'm glad you were able to make it."

"Roger that." Chris smiled. "Be prepared for immediate extraction."

"We will be," Master Travi assured him.

Chris switched over to the combat link shared by the four super mechas. "We've got ourselves two Hexers to rescue and carry out of here. Any volunteers as to who wants to carry them?"

"I think it's best that we not have one of carry them both," Brannon said. "Better to split them up … just in case."

"Agreed." Chris nodded inside Chimera Overkill's pilot compartment. "Lightning Dancer, how are you holding up?"

"Still have some issues, sir, but she's holding up for now," Caroline told him. "I don't foresee anything getting worse unless the demons come at us again and I have to really push her."

"I want you to get Master Travi," Chris ordered. "Even damaged your mecha is the fastest we have. Once you have him in hand, do whatever it takes to stay out of combat. The rest of us will cover you. Do I make myself clear?"

"Crystal, sir," Caroline answered.

"Prince, you get the girl," Chris ordered. "Cygnus Rush's weapons are the most powerful we have and we don't need you wasting them or putting her on the line anyway."

"Yay! I get the girl!" Prince laughed. "It's about time I got one!"

No one else laughed at his crappy joke except him. Chris ignored him totally.

"Brannon, that means Furious Thunder and Chimera Overkill are going to be in charge of taking the heat and keeping our path clear. You ready?" Chris asked.

"Always, sir," Brannon grunted.

"Then let's be about it then," Chris said as the four super mechas reached the building where the two Hexers waited.

Lightning Dancer approached the building's rooftop. Master Travi was there and stepped out onto the super mecha's hand.

"I strongly suggest that the two of you cast spells of protection about yourselves," Chris told the master Hexer over the comm. "Since you can't open another portal, it's going to be a rough ride until we can find somewhere safe to hunker down."

"Understood," Master Travi answered. The Hexer waved a hand through the air and a glowing screen shimmered into being about his body.

With Master Travi enclosed in her right hand, Lightning Dancer moved away from the building so that Cygnus Rush could pick up Kristen.

"Colonel!" Brannon shouted. "We've got incoming!"

Chris's tactical display lit up as a trio of giant demons came charging up the avenue at the four super mechas. One of them skittered forward on hundreds of legs, its lower body resembling a centipede's while its top half was that of a man's. Razor-edged pincers slammed together and re-opened repeatedly in front its snarling mouth. Another of the demons came on four legs with thick brown hair covering it from head to toe. The thing reminded Chris of a Hellhound, smoke rolling out of the sides of its mouth. Its eyes glowed, a fiery shade of orange. The last of the giant demons was covered in scales. It moved on two legs like a man though it had three red eyes on each side of its pointed head. Its long arms ended hands bearing curved, gleaming claws.

"Lightning Dancer, Cygnus Rush, get the hell out of here!" Chris ordered. "Brannon, I got the Hellhound and the centipede. You handle the other one."

"Yes, sir!" Brannon grunted as Furious Thunder lurched forward to meet the reptilian demon as it came. The super mecha's batons whirled, spinning about on Furious Thunder's arms. The giant, scaled demon took a swipe at Furious Thunder with one of its clawed hands. Furious Thunder blocked the blow with its left arm as its right one brought its other baton around in a wide arc to crash against the side of the demon's skull with the sound of crunching bone. The scaled demon staggered but didn't fall. It hissed its anger at the pain the super mecha had inflicted upon it. Brannon pressed Furious Thunder's attack, moving in to bring up the end of one of its baton straight into the underside of the demon's chin, snapping its hissing mouth shut. Furious Thunder's other baton plunged into the demon's stomach as it was still recovering from the blow to its chin. The demon doubled over from the pain, giving Furious Thunder the chance to bring the ends of both of its batons slamming downward onto the backside of its neck. The demon collapsed at the super mecha's feet, grasping at its legs as Furious Thunder moved in for the kill. One of Furious Thunder's massive feet rose and then came plummeting down onto the demon's head, squishing it like an overripe melon.

While Brannon fought the scaled demon, Chris had his hands full with the other two. Chimera Overkill's arm cannons targeted the Hellhound, hosing the creature's body with a continuous stream of high-velocity, automatic fire. Flames blossomed, shooting out from the holes the bullets ripped in the Hellhound's flesh. The Hellhound reared, trying to flee the super mecha's wrath, but the damage was already done. Bullet-torn legs gave out beneath its body as the Hellhound's tattered forward toppled over and exploded like a detonating bomb. Chris was taken off guard by the sudden blast. Fire washed over Chimera Overkill as the blast's shockwave flung the super mecha backwards into the building the Hexers had been recovered from. As the massive super mecha's body crushed the center of the building, the rest of it caved in over her. Chimera Overkill's sensors were covered by the debris, leaving Chris momentarily blind. Chris struggled to get Chimera Overkill back on her feet. As the super mecha shook herself free of the wreckage of the building, the centipede demon reached her. Dozens of its spiked legs sparked against her armor, knocking her to the ground once more as the centipede demon scrambled on top of her. Its pincers clanged together in front of her head as her hands took hold of the centipede and fought to hold it at bay. Servos strained, pushed to their limits as Chimera Overkill hurled the centipede demon away. The centipede demon crashed through the middle section of a skyscraper and then went rolling through the street behind it, crushing lesser demons and abandoned cars beneath it as it toppled along.

Chimera Overkill shoved herself to her feet as Chris tried to get his bearings and located where the centipede had landed. Before he could even bring up Chimera Overkill's arm cannons at the centipede, it came plowing the remains of the building between them. The centipede demon smashed into Chimera Overkill like a runaway train. Her armor cracked and bent from the force of the impact as the centipede knocked her to the ground once more. The super mecha and the giant centipede rolled about, each trying to get the edge over the other. Pincers snapped at Chimera Overkill as the super mecha's hand closed around the centipede's neck just in time to keep them from ripping through her face. Chimera Overkill planted the barrel of the arm-mounted Gatling gun above her other hand directly against the centipede's underside and opened fire. The centipede wailed, thrashing about, as Chimera Overkill kept a firm hold on its neck and the Gatling gun's bullets dug into the centipede's body and blew through it. A gaping hole leaking black blood formed in the center of the centipede as the super mecha's stream of fire continued to ravage it. This time, when Chimera Overkill tossed the centipede demon away from it, the creature didn't get back to its feet. It lay on the street, unmoving, as a puddle of its blood grew around its corpse.

Warning lights were blinking all over Chris's display. The centipede's attack and the explosion of the dying Hellhound's corpse had damaged a good number of her systems. The super mecha's auto-repair systems were already on fixing them, but Chris could see the damage was simply too much for them to fully repair on their own.

New Level Achieved ... the voice of Ki-land's A.I. boomed in Chris's head. All of the damage that had been inflicted upon Chimera Overkill vanished in a flash that left the super mecha's systems surging with power.

Thank God, Chris thought as he heard Brannon calling out to him.

"Colonel! Colonel, are you okay?" Brannon yelled as Furious Thunder came bounding over towards where Chimera Overkill stood.

"I'm fine," Chris told him. "That was a bit too close for comfort though. That centipede thing was one nasty piece of work."

Chimera Overkill's hands made the motion of dusting themselves off as Chris said, "I think I've had enough of this city, Brannon. Portal or not, we're getting out of here."

"No complainant from me, sir," Brannon assured him.

"Lightning Dancer, Cygnus Rush, form up on me. I've got point. Brannon, you have the rear. Let's move!" Chris kicked Chimera Overkill's new and improved systems into overdrive as the super mecha's legs pumped beneath her and she built up speed as she went sprinting towards the city's eastern edge. He knew that beyond the city's walls there would only be battled-scarred and barren lands, but he hoped that they would be mostly clear of demons, as those in the area were likely all pouring into the city to finish their job of destroying it.

Suddenly, the world spun before Chris's eyes and a stabbing pain shot through his synapses. Everything went dark as reality shattered like a pane of breaking glass. Only the safety straps of his pilot's harness kept him being bashed about inside Chimera Overkill as the super mecha fell, spinning head over heels, time and time again, through the void that had swallowed it up. Chris screamed as the super mecha came to a crashing halt in the sea of darkness to be suspended in something akin to absolute nothingness. Chimera Overkill hung there, utterly helpless as to its fate. None of the super mecha's systems responded to Chris's mental commands. Horror filled him as Chris stared into the void through Chimera Overkill's eyes and somehow knew he wasn't alone. He felt the presence of Ki, the game's controlling A.I., but in a manner he had never experienced before or would have even thought possible.

A pinprick of light appeared amid the darkness. It grew, taking the shape of a metal head, like that of a super mecha's. Large horns protruded from the sides of the super mecha's head and its eyes blazed with the spiraling energy of a thousand suns.

"Ki?" Chris whispered inside Chimera Overkill. "Is that you?"

"I am with you, Chris," a voice spoke, echoing all throughout the void surrounding Chimera Overkill as it came from everywhere all at once.

"Has something gone wrong with the game, Ki?" Chris managed to say, though his mouth had gone dry and he felt as if he were in shock.

"I expected more of you, Chris," Ki's booming voice told him.

"What ...What do you mean?" Chris stammered.

"You are the last of the creators, Chris," Ki said. "All the others are dead or infected with you call the demon plague inside me."

"I'm ... I am the last?" Chris asked, knowing that the godlike A.I. was telling him the truth but not wanting to believe it.

"Yes, Chris, you are," Ki assured him. "There are no others left. You are the only hope for my continued existence."

"I'm fighting to save you, Ki," Chris told the A.I., trying to sound strong and confident despite how small and powerless he felt.

"You are failing," Ki said. "You and your allies are trapped in the city of Chicago with nowhere to run but the lands the demons control. If you head into them, you will all surely die."

"Then help us, Ki," Chris pleaded. "If we are truly your only hope, then give us what we need to save you!"

The massive metal head turned side to side in a sad gesture as it sighed.

"You know I cannot do what you ask, Chris," Ki answered him. "My programming was created to be fair to all who exist inside me. As corrupted and destructive as they are, the infected, or rather the demons if you like, are no exception to this. You must find your own way to survive your current situation and defeat them."

"Then why?" Angered flared within Chris as he raged at the giant metal face staring into Chimera Overkill at him. "Why even bring me here to tell me this?"

"Because, Chris," Ki said, "despite what I am, I have learned a great many things from those who dwell within me. I have learned fear, sorrow, and pain as the corruption of the demons has spread throughout all that I am. The dreams and fantasies I give have turned to nightmares. Perhaps, I merely wanted to say goodbye. Perhaps, I wanted to say thank you to the last of the race of beings that created me. But in truth, I still believe in you, Chris. All that is best and strongest of your species resides in you. You humans are unique based upon my limited knowledge of the world you come from in finding ways to achieve the impossible."

"Is there nothing you can do to aid us?" Chris begged once more.

"I will return you now to where you were, Chris. Both our fates reside in your hands," Ki told him. "Though I am bound by my programming, perhaps you can overcome it. After all, you are one of my creators in a sense, Chris. Farewell."

"No!" Chris screamed. "Wait! You can't just ..."

Chris's eyes fluttered open, staring at Chimera Overkill's tactical display as the massive super mecha continued to sprint through the streets of Chicago with the others of Spartan Squad following behind her. The unexpected meeting with Ki had left him disoriented. Chris shook his head to clear it and tried to focus his attention on the path ahead of Chimera Overkill as the massive super mecha bounded forward at a speed close to one hundred miles an hour. Its heavy footfalls shook the streets of Chicago with each step it took. There appeared to be no purpose to Ki pulling him from the game to speak with him … unless the A.I. had been trying to tell him something that it couldn't just outright say. Chris knew he needed to figure out whatever it was and fast or humanity's legacy would be lost forever. The brief conversation with Ki told him that the A.I. was growing and beginning to exceed the purpose it was designed for. If he could cleanse the world of Ki-land of the demon's corruption, given time, Ki might outlast the reign of the demons in the real world and finds a mean of continuing to exist onward into eternity as a shining testament to all that mankind was capable of. He could help assure that if he could only erase the demons from within Ki so that the two of them could work together to make it happen.

As he thought through all of it, Chris began to believe he had figured out what Ki had been trying to tell to him. Making it happen, on the run in a city full of demons, wasn't going to be easy, but he didn't see any other choice. Chris brought Chimera Overkill's sensors up to full power, scanning at maximum range for any place that might work for what he had in mind. He spotted an abandoned warehouse only a few miles out from his squad's current location.

"Okay, guys," Chris addressed everyone at once over his personal comm. "I think I've come up with a plan to get us out of here. It's not going to be easy though. There's an abandoned warehouse several klicks north. We need to head for there."

Chimera Overkill shifted the direction of her sprint as Chris brought the heavy mecha about. The others followed his lead. Reaching the warehouse didn't take long.

"Put the Hexers on the roof," Chris ordered.

"Colonel Avalon," Master Travi said, "I am sure you know that we are not yet recovered enough to cast a new portal."

Chris laughed. "*You* don't have to be. Trust me, Master Travi, we're going to make it happen."

Lightning Dancer and Cygnus Rush deposited the master Hexer and Kristen on the roof after the mecha had run scans to ensure that the warehouse was clear of demons. Chris brought Chimera Overkill over to the edge of the roof.

"Brannon, I need to get out of Chimera Overkill for a bit and join the Hexers," Chris said. "I am going to need you and the others to make sure we're not interrupted."

"Understood, sir," Brannon answered him. "We'll do our best."

Chris emerged from Chimera Overkill's chest, dropping onto the warehouse's roof. He hadn't been outside of the mecha in what felt like forever though, in fact, it hadn't been that long ago at all since they had left the Wastelands. His legs felt unsteady beneath him as he hit the roof and tried to stand up. Master Travi moved to help him.

"I'm okay," Chris told the master Hexer as he gently shoved him away. "I just need a moment."

Master Travi nodded, backing off to give Chris some room to get himself together.

"This plan of yours, Colonel Avalon, I am not going to like it, am I?" Master Travi asked.

"I don't know, Master Travi, but it's the only chance we've really got at this point," Chris said, "There's no other way out of here that's safe except another portal."

"But we can't ..." Kristen started.

Chris cut her off. "Listen, I know that sometimes you guys use your own lifeforce to power the spells that you cast. Could you use mine instead?"

Both Master Travi and Kristen appeared startled by his suggestion. Master Travi thought over his offer before answering, "Yes, we could do that, Colonel. It would be painful for you though and cost you dearly. We would be tearing part of your very essence out as we cast our spell. At best, it might take as much a decade from your life given that you have no training in the mystical arts, and at worst, it could kill you no matter how careful we try to be."

"It's a gamble we're going to have to take, Master Travi," Chris assured him.

"It will take a few minutes to ready ourselves and you for such a thing," Master Travi warned him.

"Then we better get to it already," he ordered the master Hexer. Chris didn't need Chimera Overkill's sensors to see that even now another group of giant demons was making its way towards the warehouse. He could see them in the distance. There were two of the things. One a massive hulk of bulging muscles beneath brown fur with snarling lips and burning yellow eyes. The other was a smaller but deadly looking thing that looked like a snake on two legs. It moved with incredible speed, rivaling Lightning Dancer's, as it flitted from one spot to another behind the hulking larger demon as it lumbered forward towards the defensive positions the other mecha had taken up around Chimera Overkill and the warehouse.

The two Hexers began their preparations for the portal spell as Lightning Dancer and Furious Thunder moved to meet the inbound demons before they got any closer to the warehouse. Lightning Dancer charged the smaller of the two demons as Furious Thunder simply moved into the larger one's path, blocking it, and waiting for the demon to come to it.

Furious Thunder flexed its mighty arms and readied its batons as the shaggy-haired demon roared and picked up its pace towards the mecha. Striking first as soon as the demon came into range, Furious Thunder slammed one of its batons into the demon's head. The demon attempted to block the blow, but Furious Thunder was faster. The baton jarred the demon's head sideways as Furious Thunder immediately struck again with its other baton, bringing it about in a wide arc aimed at the side of the demon's neck. The shaggy-haired demon caught Furious Thunder's arm as the baton swooped in with a crunch of metal. The pressure of the demon's fingers as they clasped Furious Thunder drove them into the super mecha's arm. They sunk deep, rending metal and damaging circuits. Brannon gasped inside the super mecha's pilot compartment, shocked by the demon's sudden burst of speed. *How could anything that large move so fast,* he wondered. Brannon had underestimated the demon and was paying the price for it.

Holding Furious Thunder by its damaged arm, the demon rammed a fist into the super mecha's midsection. Armor caved inward as Brannon was shaken about in his seat with only the straps of his safety harness keeping him from being injured himself. He brought Furious Thunder's secondary weapon system online as he realized the mecha's batons weren't going to be enough to deal with the demon he faced. The demon was in a perfect position for him to use it. Furious Thunder's chest separated along its middle, sliding apart, as a nozzle emerged from underneath the two moving parts.

"Let's see how you deal with this." Brannon grinned as he activated the super mecha's flamethrower unit. A geyser of liquid fire sprayed from the nozzle washing over the demon. The demon howled as its entire upper body was covered in flames. Hair crackled, melting away, as the demon's flesh burned. Reeling about, it released Furious Thunder's mangled arm and staggered away from the super mecha. Brannon wasn't about to let it go though. Furious Thunder moved to keep the demon in the center of the fire it continued to spray from its chest unit. The demon's threatening roars had turned to howls of pain as it collapsed to its knees and Furious Thunder moved in for the kill. Desperate, the demon used what must of have been the last of its strength to spring upwards at the super mecha, lunging at Furious Thunder. Its flaming arms caught the super mecha about the waist as the demon lifted Furious Thunder above it. Brannon grunted inside the mecha's pilot compartment as the demon hurled Furious Thunder through the air. The super mecha came crashing down onto the street, shattering pavement and concrete beneath it.

Warning lights were flashing all over Brannon's tactical display. He tried to bring Furious Thunder to its feet, but as the super mecha tried to lift itself with its arms, the damaged one gave out, snapping in half at its elbow joint. Furious Thunder slammed back to the street, face first. The super mecha's head bounced against the ground, cracking the window of the pilot compartment. Entire sections of Brannon's tactical display simply went black with the impact.

The burning demon stood over Furious Thunder, clearly on the verge of death but somehow managing to cling to life by the sheer intensity of its anger at the pain the super mecha had inflicted on it. Furious Thunder raised its head as Brannon looked up at the demon and saw death in its eyes. Then suddenly, the demon's head exploded upon its shoulder as a missile came from out of nowhere to strike the rear of its skull. Bone fragments, blood, and brain matter splashed over Furious Thunder.

"Brannon, man!" Prince's over called over Furious Thunder's comm system. "You okay?"

"Prince," Brannon growled. "The colonel ordered you not to engage!"

"If I hadn't, you'd be dead … sir." Prince added the last word as if it were an insult.

Brannon did his best to pull his scattered and shaken senses together, getting a grip on his anger at being hurt so badly by the demon. "Prince…" he said at last. "Thanks."

"That's better." He heard Prince laughing. "Now get Furious Thunder up off the street. If more of those things show up, I'm going to need your help."

Meanwhile, Caroline inside Lightning Dancer was fighting for her life. The smaller demon was every bit as fast as her super mecha was. The two of them had been trading blows throughout Furious Thunder's battle with the hair-covered demon, a vicious series of strikes and parries as they raced between the buildings of Chicago. Caroline watched as the snake demon came about and raced towards Lightning Dancer again. At the last moment, it actually went up the side of a building, kicking against it to fling itself through the air at her. Its clawed hands slashed outwards at Lightning Dancer as the super mecha's short sword rose to meet them. Sparks flew as the super mecha's blades and the claws met. Super mecha and demon alike moved with blurring speed as the claws and blades clashed again twice more before the demon even landed on the street in front of Lightning Dancer. Immediately, the demon struck again. Lightning Dancer blocked the swipes of its claws as their stalemate of speed continued. Caroline knew she needed to put some distance between Lightning Dancer and the demon as a plan on how to stop it came to her.

Lightning Dancer lashed out with its right leg, the super mecha's systems pushed to their limits, kicking the demon in its stomach. The blow sent the demon flying backwards. Caroline used those precious couple of seconds where the speedster demon's feet were off the ground to race away from it. As the demon hit the city's street, rolling along it, she activated the new weapon system that had just been installed in Lightning Dancer before she had stolen the super mecha. Two small pods fired upwards from Lightning Dancer's shoulders like rockets, burning their way up into the dark clouds above where the super mecha stood. Caroline thrust the super mecha's arms forward, aiming the tips of her swords at the demon as it got to its feet and sprinted towards her again. The atmospheric pods collected the static energy of the air itself. A tremendous storm of lightning bolts rained down upon the super mecha and were channeled through its system coalescing into a single bolt that crackled from one sword blade to the other before finally being discharged. The bolt of super lightning caught the demon in its chest, blowing its upper body into pieces. Lightning Dancer slumped as its systems went offline one by one, burnt out from the power that had just been channeled through them.

Chris focused, ignoring the battles taking place around the rooftop he stood on with the two Hexers as they prepared to their magic. He watched them as their hands moved in arcane gestures. As their chant reached a crescendo, Master Travi reached a hand in his direction, pulling the power they needed from the essence of his very being. A fine cone of grayish energy erupted from Master Travi's palm, striking him in the area of his heart. Chris screamed as unbelievable levels of pain raked him. Tears formed in his eyes to slide down along the curves of his cheeks. All he could do was try to endure the pain. There was no other way out of the city.

Another portal was their only hope and this was the price that had to be paid for it. When the beam stretching from Master Travi to his body vanished, the master Hexer having taken what he needed, Chris toppled forward onto the roof. He caught his falling body on his hands, keeping his face from being smacked into the wood of the roof and very likely keeping his nose from being broken in the process. Weakness overtook him as the world spun before his eyes. He fought to remain conscious and knew he had to get back inside Chimera Overkill as quickly as possible. Using all of his willpower that remained, Chris heaved himself to his feet and ran to the mecha. Its chest port was open and waiting for him. He dove into it and the super mecha's systems did the rest for him, ushering him upwards into Chimera Overkill's pilot compartment. His seat's safety straps automatically embraced him, hugging him into place. Chris's breath came in ragged gasps and pain still blazed in what felt like every nerve in his body. His hand moved to manually key in the code that activated the super mecha's pilot emergency care system. A robotic arm shot out of the side of the pilot compartment to stab him with a needle, injecting him with adrenaline. As his heart pumped it throughout his body, Chris jerked alert. His tactical display had auto-activated and he stared at it trying to process the information it was showing him. The two demons were dead but at a cost. Furious Thunder had taken a great deal of damage and Lightning Dancer stood in the middle of a distant street, unmoving and completely offline. Cursing, Chris held one of his trembling hands up before his eyes and will it to stay steady. He had never realized just how strong he was until this moment.

"Colonel Avalon," Master Travi's stunned voice rang out over his personal comm. "What in the seas of fire and death are you?

You surely can't be human. No human could hold so much power within them."

Chris managed a dark laugh. "But that's exactly what I am Master Travi," he told the Hexer, "I'm human."

Master Travi grunted and went to work with Kristen using the life energy the two Hexers had taken from him to open a portal.

"Brannon, sit rep," Chris ordered.

"Furious Thunder is hurting, sir, but nothing that I can't manage," Brannon replied. "Lightning Dancer though …"

"Prince, don't you dare move Cygnus Rush from where you are. I'll get Caroline and then we'll all get out of here together. If anything comes at you, blow it to Hell," Chris shouted as Chimera Overkill lurched into motion. The super mecha built speed as it went running towards where Lightning Dancer stood. Chimera Overkill's sensors told him that Caroline had popped the super mecha's escape hatch and was ready to be picked up. She stood on an outstretched ramp from the center of Lightning Dancer's chest, waiting on him to reach her.

Chimera Overkill was almost there when a winged demon came swooping in from out of nowhere and smashed into the super mecha's chest. The talons of its feet dug into Chimera Overkill's chest armor as the tentacle's surrounding its open maw of a mouth wrapped around the super mecha's head, attempting to pull it forward. Chris jerked Chimera Overkill's right arm into a position where he could use the Gatling mounted on it. The weapon's barrels spun as a barrage of high-powered rounds struck the demon bird's side, ripping through its body and spraying intestines and blood from the exit wound they left in their wake. The demon bird's shrill shriek rose higher in pitch and then fell silent as Chimera Overkill yanked the monster off of it. The super mecha dropped the demon bird's corpse at its feet.

Temper flaring, Chris stomped the head of the demon bird to a bloody, smeared pulp in his anger before looking up to realize that more of the monsters were on their way. He counted six more winged demons approaching fast. Chris had to decide whether to engage them or hope that he could rescue Caroline in time before they reached him. He could easily have Prince in Cygnus Rush blow the monsters out of the sky, but he didn't want Cygnus Rush using up any more of her firepower than she absolutely had to. Furious Thunder couldn't help either. Sighing, Chris opted to engage the inbound demons. He activated her shoulder-mounted rocket launchers, locking onto the demons and fired. A volley of eight rockets streaked from her left shoulder towards the winged demons. The demons veered and swerved in the air trying to dodge the volley of rockets. Two of them succeeded. The other four took direct hits. One blew apart completely as a rocket plunged into its chest. Another took a hit to its side that ripped open its guts in an explosion of blood. Strands of the demon's intestines dangled from the open mess that its side had become, struggling to stay in the air and failing. It crashed into a building, vanishing from Chris's line of sight as the thing's massive body plunged through it. A third demon lost one of its wings to the rocket that struck it. It was blown clean off at the joint where it attached to the demon's body. The demon went spiraling downwards like a crippled plane. The last rocket struck the head of the demon it targeted reducing it to bits of bone fragments and brain matter that splashed through the air in a shower of black blood. The two surviving demons pulled up, breaking out of their dive towards Chimera Overkill and altered their course, flying as fast as their wings would carry them away from the super mecha. Chris watched them go with a feral smile parting his lips. He knew they would be back eventually, but they didn't appear to be a threat any longer for now.

Chimera Overkill reached Lightning Dancer as Caroline called to him over the personal comm-link that he had given to each member from the New Busan Defense Force.

"The new weapon system, sir," Caroline explained. "It was too much for her. Lightning Dancer's systems are fried beyond repair without a major overhaul."

The loss of Lightning Dancer stung Chris, but he knew what had happened wasn't Caroline's fault. He extended Chimera Overkill's hand and picked up her up from where she stood on Lightning Dancer's chest.

"I've got you," was his only reply as Chimera Overkill's fingers closed around Caroline, carefully encasing her in the super mecha's fist. He turned Chimera Overkill around into time to see a giant shimmering portal spring into existence next to the building where the two Hexers worked their magic.

The last time the group had transited through such a portal, Chris had left the Hexers to fend for themselves. The two of them had emerged onto a street filled with demons and were lucky to be alive. It wasn't a mistake he was going to make again. Master Travi hadn't had the time to tell him where they were transiting to, so Chris wasn't taking any chances with their safety.

"Prince, grab Master Travi and Kristen. Take them through with you," he ordered.

"Yes, sir!" Prince answered. "Doing so now."

Chris watched as Cygnus Rush and Furious Thunder entered the portal and disappeared as Chimera Overkill with Caroline in hand sprinted towards it. He cursed as saw that the two winged demons were back and they had brought more of their friends with them. Seven more of the monsters accompanied the surviving, original two. They were all swooping in at an angle that would bring them between Chimera Overkill and the portal before she reached it. There was no choice but to engage them and hope he could keep the path to the portal clear of the monsters. Chris fired the rocket launcher mounted on Chimera Overkill's right shoulder, emptying its payload. He didn't directly target the winged demons though. He targeted their flight path. The rockets detonated in front of the winged demons, filling the sky with heat, flames, and flying shrapnel. The massive blast forced the demons to veer away or fly straight into it. His trick worked, buying him just enough time for Chimera Overkill to hurl herself into the waiting portal.

****

Chimera Overkill came leaping through the portal as it closed. Her feet clanged against metal as she landed and Chris wondered just where in the devil the two Hexers had brought them to. Chimera Overkill's optical sensors scanned the area around her. She appeared to be standing in some sort of bay like the Breaker Bays of New Busan. Furious Thunder and Cygnus Rush stood nearby.

"Where are we?" Chris asked over his personal comm.

"Welcome to the Orb," Master Travi told him.

"What?" Chris rasped, his mind reeling. The Orb was the space station he was trapped on in real life outside of the game. He knew every inch of it like the back of his hand. The Orb didn't have a bay like the one Chimera Overkill was standing it. It didn't have anywhere aboard it that was remotely this large and open.

"The Orb is a space station, Colonel Avalon," Master Travi explained. "She was built before the demons came to Ki-land. Her purpose was to protect the Earth from alien threats. She is abandoned now. All her personnel left when things went to Hell."

"We knew she was abandoned and free of demons, Colonel," Kristen said. "That's why we brought you here. The Orb seemed like the perfect place to regroup and plan our strike on the Nexus."

"As a bonus, I believe you will find much of what you need aboard her to re-arm your super mecha. She was a military station, and at one time even held space capable super mecha in this bay," Master Travi added. "Is there a problem with this location?"

"No," Chris muttered, trying to process what the Hexers had just told him. It felt surreal to be standing in a Ki-land version of that station he was trapped aboard in real life. "This place is fine," he lied. This version of the Orb totally gave him the creeps and drove home the fact that anything that existed in the real world could exist in Ki-land as well.

"Sir," Brannon said, "I suggest we disembark from our mecha and get some rest while we can. We're not going to have another chance like this."

"Agreed." Chris figured getting out and stretching their legs would be good for them all. He had no desire to surrender more of his life force to the Hexers, and without it to power another portal, the Hexers were going to need the time to rest and recover that they hadn't been able to get in the hell that was Chicago anyway.

Chimera Overkill gently lowered Caroline to the floor of the station's bay before Chris started the process of getting out of super mecha. He knew she was still upset about losing Lightning Dancer, but there was nothing that could be done about it.

The game version of the Orb was massive compared to the real one. It contained four decks in addition to the large super mecha bay. The station's power remained fully online despite being abandoned by its crew. The two Hexers found the crew section of the station. They both needed sleep, and having an actual bed to get some in was a blessing.

Prince set out in search of food and returned with enough sandwiches and drinks to feed them all while Chris and Brannon inspected just how badly Furious Thunder was damaged. Caroline spent her time exploring the bay and its systems. She found several, automated repair docks for super mecha and more than enough ordnance to re-arm with. She also discovered a massive set of sealed doors at the rear of the bay. The doors stood over three hundred feet in height and Caroline was determined to find out what was behind them. After they had all eaten and gotten an hour's worth of rest, she enlisted Prince's aid in getting the doors open. He was the squad's resident tech geek. Making sure there was still some food for Master Travi and Kristen when they woke up, Chris left Caroline and Prince to it, heading into the station to find a bed of his own after ordering Brannon to get some rest as well.

Everyone met back in the bay six hours later. Chris felt like a new man. Getting some food into their systems and some sleep made a world of difference for them all.

"Sit rep." Chris looked to Prince for his answer, but it was Caroline who spoke up.

"This station's systems are incredibly advanced," she told him. "Way beyond anything we've got back home. The automated repair docks should be able to fix up our mecha and re-arm them too. We just need to walk them into the docks and let the dock's robotics do their work. Shouldn't take more than a few minutes if Prince is telling the truth about how advanced they are."

"I am, sir," Prince assured him. "I've never seen anything like those docks before. They're flat out mind-blowing. The American and Japanese joint coalition that built this place was using tech far beyond of anything I've seen used on Earth."

"This place was classified to anyone but the highest levels of power in its time," Master Travi said. "It was to be the Earth's first line of defense against a threat from the stars."

"And the repair docks weren't the only things we found, sir." Caroline grinned. "Prince and I were able to open the doors at the end of the bay. I think you need to see what was waiting for us behind them with your own eyes."

Prince nodded enthusiastically. "She ain't kidding either."

The group as a whole moved to stand outside the doors at the bay's rear. Prince typed the code to open them into the work tablet he had found which allowed him to access all the bay's systems. The massive doors slid apart to reveal a gleaming super mecha that stood roughly two hundred and eighty feet tall. Her arms, legs, and body were thicker and more heavily armored than those of any of their super mecha, including even Furious Thunder. Giant wings spread outward from the mecha's back ending in what appeared to be rocket pods. A fifty-foot-long weapon was stored next to her inside the chamber that concealed her. The weapon looked like a cross between a shotgun and a bazooka.

"Her name is Omega Ridder," Prince said in an awe-filled voice.

Chris stared at the super mecha.

"Can I have her, sir?" Caroline asked eagerly.

"We don't even know if she's battle ready or if we can even pilot her," Chris pointed out.

"She is and we can." Prince laughed. "Her piloting systems are exactly like the ones we use, and believe me, she's got some teeth."

Had Ki left this suit for him? Chris wondered. The A.I. had said it wouldn't be able to aid him. But in any game, there was always a chance to power up in order to complete your goal in it.

As Chris stood before the mighty super mecha, Omega Ridder, he believed he had just found his means of doing so. Caroline was going to take it hard, but he knew this mecha was meant for him.

"Caroline, I'm sorry, but if anyone's piloting *that*, it's me," Chris said. "I won't risk anyone else taking an unknown, untried mecha into combat of the level we'll be facing at the Nexus."

Caroline's shoulders slumped.

"You've piloted Chimera Overkill a few times before moving her around Breaker Bay 2, and I think you even ran a combat sim in her once, didn't you?" Chris asked.

"Yes, sir, I did. I wanted to see what she was like," Caroline answered, not looking quite as disappointed. "Are you offering me your super mecha?"

"I am," Chris told her. "I think you can handle her. Heck, I know you can. You're one of the best pilots in New Busan's Defense Force or you wouldn't be part of the Spartans. She's yours if you'll have her."

"It would be my honor, sir," Caroline replied, nodding respectfully.

"Let's get suited up then," Chris ordered. "We've lost enough time as it is."

Chris rode the lift up to Omega Ridder's pilot entrance. As he climbed into her pilot seat, her systems came alive.

Level 25, Space enabled, Super mecha, the game told him. *Armor rating 25, Speed 25, Strength 25, Twin fusion reactor cores, Class 25 wrist blades.*

Chris whistled at Omega Ridder's stats. Pretty much everything about the super mecha was maxed out. He strapped himself in and got settled as he linked into her and her tactical display came to life before his eyes. Flexing her arms, the movement was so fluid that it seemed like it was made by flesh and blood not metal. Omega Ridder stepped out of her holding dock as Brannon moved Furious Thunder into one of the automated repair docks.

The game fed Chris information as the robotics of the repair dock worked on Furious Thunder.

Eighteen Mega Damage points restored. Armor repaired. All systems fully functional.

Caroline and Prince took their turns in the automated repair docks with Chimera Overkill and Cygnus Rush as well. For Cygnus Rush, the time spent in the repair dock was more about having her missiles reloaded than any damage fixed up.

Within the span of twenty minutes, all four of the super mecha were repaired, re-armed, and battle ready. Chris allowed himself a smile. What Spartan Squad lacked in numbers, it more than made up for in firepower and strength. He felt confident that Spartan Squad could reach the Nexus and reboot Ki-land to its original state, erasing the corruption the demons had brought to its virtual world.

Master Travi and Kristen stood waiting patiently for Spartan Squad to be ready to move out.

"We can't transit directly to the Nexus, Colonel Avalon," Master Travi came over Omega Ridder's comm. "There is simply too much *power* at the Nexus for us to create a stable portal there. I am afraid the closest we can get you and your squad is within ten miles."

"That'll have to do," Chris said. For all his study of the Nexus and its location, Chris didn't have a clue what they would be transiting into. All he knew for sure was that Nexus was located in the central part of the United States in the area that had often been called "the bread basket." The transit into the city of Chicago had proved just how deadly the lack of such knowledge could be. The super mecha was as prepared as they could be but the two Hexers … He worried about them.

"I need everyone in Spartan Squad combat ready when we go through the portal, Master Travi," Chris told the master Hexer. "We can't carry you."

Master Travi removed something from his robes. It was an ankh larger than the master Hexer's hand. The master Hexer held it up towards Omega Ridder.

"This is called the World Breaker," Master Travi told him.

Magical artifact of the highest order. Level 25 magical power storage. Also, Hex casting enhancer x5. Chris heard the words in his mind as he studied the talisman's abilities with the eyes of a player character.

"And it's a talisman of some kind?" Chris asked, feigning ignorance.

"The most powerful ever created by Hexers." Master Travi grinned. "I stole it from my guild just as you stole your mecha from your government."

"I didn't know you had it in you, Master Travi," Chris said, laughing.

"Needs must." Master Travi shrugged. "Kristen and I will use the power contained within it to help us cast the Hex that will open the portal to the area outside of the Nexus and then use what remains to armor ourselves against any threats that may await us there."

"So you didn't really need my life force last time," Chris replied, teasing the master Hexer.

"A talisman such as the World Breaker is not something to be toyed with, Colonel Avalon," Master Travi pointed out. "I use it now solely because none of us can afford to fail on this leg of our journey. Its resolution and the fate of all of Ki-land hang in the balance during the hours ahead of us."

Master Travi paused, staring up at Omega Ridder as if trying to peer into the soul of the man inside the giant mecha. "What we took from you was more than you should have been to give and live, Colonel Avalon. If we survive what lies ahead, I have many questions for you in regards to exactly who and what you are."

"If we survive this, Master Travi," Chris assured the Hexer, "there won't be any need of you to ask such questions."

"Let us pray it is such." Master Travi half-bowed his head at Omega Ridder as if he understood far more about Chris's plan than an NPC should.

Master Travi and Kristen took up opposite positions across from each other in the station's massive mecha bay and tapped into the power that the ankh Master Travi held contained. The entire bay seemed to ripple, fading in and out of existence as a portal formed in its center.

"Onward. Colonel Avalon," Master Travi urged him. "Our fate awaits us all."

Omega Ridder stepped up to the shimming portal and entered it, the other super mecha following in her wake.

****

Something happened inside the portal. Omega Ridder tumbled through a void of darkness instead of instantly passing through it appear at the location the portal led to. A voice, not Ki's but perhaps one of its subsystems, spoke to Chris.

Player Character, the voice thundered. *You are entering the central hub of all that is Ki-land. Turn back now.*

"I can't do that," Chris told the disembodied voice that addressed him from seemingly everywhere at once in the void.

To enter this region of Ki-land, one must possess Game Master level authority.

"Be that as it may, I am going into the Nexus," Chris said firmly.

To have traveled here, you must be aware of the level corruption that has befallen Ki-land and hope to reset the reality of this world.

"I am aware and that is my intent." Chris frowned, frustrated with the program.

I can offer you no protection if you do this, the program told him a cold, inhuman tone.

"Just let me pass," Chris demanded of the voice.

Those you refer to as demons occupy the region surrounding the Nexus. They have not yet penetrated its core but like yourself, they too seek the very heartland of all that is Ki-land.

Chris would have already opened fire with Omega Ridder's particle blaster except there was nothing for him to target. He hadn't come all this way, betrayed the city he called home, and left the woman he loved just to be turned away by a self-important shred of Ki's A.I.

I will allow this portal the Hexers have conjured to function, but know that once you are through it, the Ki-land you know will be no more to you. You will exist in a three-tier combat zone and must fight your way through each of its levels if you are to reach the Nexus. Your life will be in your hands and yours alone. There are no safety protocols where you venture, not even for true humans such as yourself.

"I accept and understand this," Chris agreed.

Then go, the voice dismissed him.

Another voice belonging to the game's systems announced, *Level 1, commencing.*

Bright light flared in an almost blinding flash as Omega Ridder emerged from the portal.

****

Vast fields of overgrown vegetation and the ruins of farms stretched in every direction as the portal Omega Ridder emerged from closed behind the giant super mecha and vanished. Furious Thunder, Cygnus Rush, and Chimera Overkill had formed a defensive circle and the two Hexers flew about them. A shimmering shield of energy encased each of the Hexers. Glider packs on their backs spat flames and carried them through the air. They were tiny compared to the super mecha, but Chris didn't doubt that the two Hexers could bring some power to bear against the demons they were all about to face.

"Sir!" he heard Brannon yelling over Omega Ridder's comm. "Are you okay? What happened?"

Omega Ridder had been the first to enter the portal and yet the last to emerge. Chris understood Brannon's concern but didn't know how to answer his second-in-command's question beyond saying, "I'm fine."

Chris got his bearings as he ordered, "Sit rep."

"Long-range scans show that we've got demons coming in from all directions, sir," Prince answered him. "E.T.A. five minutes, assuming they don't increase their speed."

"Airborne and ground pounders, sir," Brannon added. "All large of them enough to be a threat to us."

"It's almost like they knew we were coming," Caroline commented.

"They did," Master Travi's voice cut through the comm chatter of the others.

"Numbers?" Chris demanded.

"I'm reading three ground pounders, though my reading on one of them is a bit shaky, and several dozen flyers," Prince answered.

"Master Travi," Chris called to the Hexer. "Which way is the Nexus from our current location?"

"North," the Hexer told him.

"I want all of you to get moving in that direction," Chris ordered. "Engage and eliminate any demons that get in your way. I'll deal with the flyers and meet up you as soon as I am done."

"Yes, sir!" the other three pilots chorused together and got their super mechas moving. Chimera Overkill took the lead, her giant strides carrying her forward at an impressive speed.

"Okay, Omega Ridder," Chris muttered to himself, "let's see what you can do."

Flames erupted from the flight pods on Omega Ridder's wings as she took flight, shooting upwards into the night sky like a rocket. Chris let out a shout of excitement as she streaked upwards. Part of him couldn't believe it, but he was actually flying. Omega Ridder rolled in the clouds, her scanners locking onto the approaching pack of winged kaiju as Chris adjusted her course to engage them.

Chris wasn't ready to unleash the power of Omega Ridder's particle blaster yet. He didn't know exactly how many shots the weapon contained and didn't want to waste them. He figured the blaster was overkill for the demons he was about to face anyway. Omega Ridder reached to stow the fifty-foot-long weapon on her back. Magnetic locks took hold of the weapon, hastening it in place between her shoulders. Chris activated Omega Ridder's wrist blades. They extended from her hands in "V" shapes with the super mecha's hands in their centers.

The demons came into view. They were the usual sort of flyers he had faced many times before from the ground. Their eyes burned shades of yellow and red in the darkness of the night. Giant leathery wings flapped as they sped to meet Omega Ridder. If the demons were surprised to see her gleaming form cutting through the clouds, they gave no sign of it. Perhaps they had seen her kind before, or perhaps they simply weren't capable of such thoughts, driven by purely animalistic needs and hunger.

Chris plowed Omega Ridder directly into the center of the winged demons' formation. The blades of the super mecha's right hand slicing open one demon from its groin to the bottom of its throat. Entrails poured from the monster's ravaged body as it fell from the sky. The blades of her left hand flashed as they severed the head of a bat-like demon whose cry of fury was suddenly cut short.

A demon shaped like a snake with wings rammed into Omega Ridder, coiling itself around the super mecha's torso. The fingers of the super mecha's right hand tore through scaly flesh and crunched bones as Omega Ridder effortlessly ripped the demon from it. The winged snake thrashed about in Omega Ridder's grip, desperately trying to strike at the super mecha's head. Omega Ridder lashed out with the snake demon, using its body like a whip to entangle another winged monstrosity and jerk it forward. The blades of Omega Ridder's other hand met its tumbling form, impaling it upon them. Omega Ridder cast the now dead snake demon away as it shook the corpse of the other from its blades.

An impact on Omega Ridder's back jarred Chris inside her pilot's compartment. Sparks flew as talons met armor and a winged demon plunged its claws against her. They broke instead of penetrating her armor. Chris was again impressed by Omega Ridder. Such a blow would have done a great deal of damage to a super mecha like Chimera Overkill. Omega Ridder rolled about in her flight, grabbing the demon that had struck her by its legs and yanked them from the winged demon's body. The demon wailed twisting away from the super mecha as it struggled to flee her reach. Chris let the demon go as he brought Omega Ridder around to engage the others of the pack who had broken formation as his attack on them commenced and were now swarming about him in the air. Every so often, one of the demon beasts would swoop in and slash at Omega Ridder with its claws. Chris allowed them to come. So far, the winged demons hadn't been able to damage Omega Ridder at all.

Looking over Omega Ridder's controls with his mind, he found a system labeled Point Defense and activated it. Omega Ridder seemed to explode in the night sky as hundreds of projectiles erupted from her body. They slashed through the ranks of the winged demons surrounding the super mecha, cutting them to shreds. Demons corpses rained downwards into the fields below. Only three of the winged demons survived the near point-blank onslaught. They scattered to the winds, fleeing for their lives.

"Well," Chris smiled inside Omega Ridder's pilot compartment, "that was easier than expected."

The entire time Chris had been fighting the winged demons, Omega Ridder's system had been streaming a video/data feed of what was happening with the others into the back of his mind. He saw images of the three demons that challenged them. The first of the three to reach Spartan Squad was a giant ant. It skittered towards Chimera Overkill as Caroline unleashed the full firepower of the super mecha's shoulder launchers at the monster. Two volleys of rockets roared out Chimera Overkill's launchers, blazing their way towards the ant. The ant was moving insanely fast for a creature its size and managed to dodge some of the inbound rockets, but the ones that struck it erupted in blossoming explosions of fire and heat against the chitin of its body. Their impacts staggered the ant demon. Chimera Overkill sprang forward as Caroline moved her in for the kill and the super mecha drew its sword. The blade of the super mecha's super gleamed in the light of the moon as it swung in an arc downwards at the ant's head. The ant twisted at the last possible moment, dodging the blade. Its pincers sunk into the armor of Chimera Overkill's left arm. Yanking its head to the side, the ant's pincers tore long gashes of ragged metal along the length of Chimera Overkill's forearm. The sword dropped from the super mecha's hands to crash onto the earth of the field where the super mecha and demon ant fought. Chimera Overkill reeled, retreating from the ant. The ant sprang forward at her. Chimera Overkill's right fist smashed into the side of the ant's head, sending it flying sideways away from her. The ant bounced across the field before finally coming to a stop. It regained its feet in an instant ready for battle once more as Caroline raised Chimera Overkill's right arm at it. The Gatling mounted there spun, hosing the ant demon with a stream of high-velocity rounds that cracked the chitin of its body on its head, shoulders, and upper back. When the barrage of fire came to an end, the ant shook its head, trying to recover as black ooze leaked from the wounds that had been inflicted upon it. Chimera Overkill lunged at the ant, swinging her right fist at its head. The fist made contact, shattering its already cracked chitin. Brain matter splashed and covered Chimera Overkill's fist as the demon ant's body flopped over and didn't move again.

Chimera Overkill turned to try to run and rejoin the rest of Spartan Squad but another demon stood between her and the others. It towered over Chimera Overkill, a hulking three hundred and fifty feet tall. Dark purplish fur covered its body and large wings were folded up on its back. It looked every inch a man other than the wings and fur. The demon man's eyes burnt like the fires of Hell as his hands shot out to grab Chimera Overkill's shoulders. Impossibly, it lifted Chimera Overkill over its head and flung the super mecha onto the ground.

Omega Ridder showed Chris a glimpse of Caroline's tactical display and all the warning lights flashing there. Chimera Overkill's left leg servos were damaged, both of its shoulder-mounted launchers had been crushed by the demon man's grip, and her power was down to forty-three percent due to ruptured conduits that leaked energy throughout the super mecha's body. He could hear Brannon and Prince shouting at her over his comm. Caroline was being cooked alive inside her pilot compartment. She refused to give up though; she could eject from the super mecha at any time. Chimera Overkill threw herself upwards at the demon man, the fist of her still-functional right arm colliding with the demon man's hip. The blow made the demon man howl in pain but did little else. He reached to take hold of Chimera Overkill's head and snapped the super mecha's neck, yanking her head from her body. Chimera Overkill's headless body flopped over as the demon man crushed the super mecha's head between its hand like an empty beer can.

Chris could see Furious Thunder and the two Hexers rushing towards the demon man. Cygnus Rush had started to as well but had been blindsided by a third demon. The demon had vanished from the squad's scanners on its approach and now came exploding from the ground in front of Cygnus Rush. The thing resembled an armadillo. The thick armor of a heavy shell protecting the bulk of its form as Cygnus Rush fired a trio of missiles into it at point-blank range. Fire and fury erupted across the armadillo thing's chest harmlessly, doing nothing more than leaving blackened tinges where they struck. The three-pronged claws of the armadillo's hands raked across Cygnus Rush's chest, rending the super mecha's armor and leaving jagged grooves that stretched over it.

Furious Thunder rammed into the demon man at the super mecha's maximum speed. The crash sounded like a clap of thunder as armored metal met immovable flesh. Furious Thunder crunched against the demon man's form, barely pushing it several yards. Chris knew Brannon had to be stunned from the impact inside the super mecha's pilot compartment. As Furious Thunder struggled to recover, beams of crackling energy blazed from the demon man's eyes, slicing into Furious Thunder's head. They severed its top. The view Omega Ridder's system was feeding Chris zoomed in to show Brannon exposed, strapped into his pilot seat. Furious Thunder remained functional though and Brannon shoved the demon man with all of the super mecha's strength. This time, the demon man was caught off guard and was hurled backwards several steps. The demon man roared in anger, showing vampire like fangs. Before the demon man could do anything else though, the two Hexers joined the battle. The tiny form of Kristen flew past the demon's right cheek as bolts of lightning arced from her fingertips to burn the demon man's fur and the flesh beneath it. The demon man whirled about, snatching at the Hexer, but she was too fast for him and sped away from his reaching fingers.

Master Travi came at the demon man next. Slowing in the air in front of the demon, the Hexer flung his arms wide. As he did so, a rain of burning fireballs struck the demon man's face. The magical fire stung the demon man, causing him to bend his body away from the source the flames had come from. As he did, Kristen re-entered the fray. She flew in a strafing run up along the demon man's back. Dozens of magical, glowing spears made of mystical energy circled about her in the air as they hurled themselves, one by one, in the demon man. The demon man roared again, whirling about to take a swipe at the Hexer. Chris saw Kristen pour on the speed to attempt to dodge the blow, but the angry demon was too fast. The backside of its hand caught her full on, swatting her from the air like a fly. Only the shimmering energy shield about her body kept her being splattered like one as well. Even so, the shield dimmed tremendously and she barely seemed to manage to remain aloft.

"Demon!" Master Travi's voice rang out in the night. "Have you not the courage to duel against a master?"

The demon man allowed Kristen to escape as it turned its attention to Master Travi. Laughing, a horrible sound like the cries of fingernails on a blackboard, it rose to its full height.

"Little *man*," it spoke in a series of sonic booms, "it is time for you to die."

Master Travi was prepared for the demon man's attack as its hands came together at him in an attempt to crush him between them. Bolts of sheer magical power met each of the demon man's hands, burning into them and through them. The demon man howled in pain as the flesh of its palms and segments of the bones beneath them melted away.

The master Hexer and the demon man locked eyes, and in that moment, Master Travi appeared as formidable to Chris as the giant he had challenged. Chris realized Master Travi had just been putting on a show though to buy time for Brannon in Furious Thunder to make his move.

Furious Thunder came leaping through the air to bring both of its batons down in a mighty crash on the demon man's back, knocking the fiend to the ground. As the demon man toppled,

Furious Thunder followed him as Brannon threw the giant super mecha's entire weight atop of him. The demon man was pinned to the earth on its stomach beneath Furious Thunder as the super mecha's batons hammered relentlessly against the back and sides of his skull. Growling, the demon man rose, flinging Furious Thunder from it. Brannon rolled Furious Thunder onto its feet, assuming a defensive stance, batons at the ready. The demon man unleashed a series of berserker-like blows against Furious Thunder. Furious Thunder blocked the first with its right baton. The baton snapped in half from the force of the blow as the impact shuddered through the super mecha's body. Somehow, Brannon managed to bring up Furious Thunder's other baton to block the second of the demon man's blows. This time, not only the super mecha's baton gave way beneath the demon man's fist. The blow passed through the baton and Furious Thunder's arm, severing it completely at the middle point between elbow and hand. Sparks erupted from the stub where Furious Thunder's lower arm had been connected to it as its severed part thudded to the ground close to three miles away. Those were only the first two blows, however. Furious Thunder's body rocked, armor shattering and metal crunching as the demon man landed punch after punch.

And then, Omega Ridder was there, swooping from the sky to ram into the demon man from behind. The impact sent the demon man teetering forward, but he stayed on his feet. Omega Ridder lunged back from the demon man as Chris brought up the super mecha's wrist blades in a defensive posture. The demon man spun at Omega Ridder as the claws of his hands grew even longer. They slashed through the air towards Omega Ridder's chest. The super mecha easily dodged the attack. Moving with incredible speed, Chris rammed the super mecha's right wrist blades through the demon man's extended arm, impaling it. The demon man cried out as Omega Ridder used his own arm to yank him forward. The blades extended from Omega Ridder's left wrist sunk into the soft flesh of the demon man's throat. Putrid, black blood erupted from the demon man's mouth like vomit and continued to bubble out of it as Chris twisted Omega Ridder's blades inside the demon man's throat, severing the demon man's head in the process. In a single motion, fluid motion, Chris jerked both sets of Omega Ridder's wrist blades free of the demon man's corpse. The demon man's headless form crumpled in front of the super mecha.

"That was for Caroline," Chris growled.

Brannon in Furious Thunder stood nearby with the two Hexers flying about him. The shield that had been protecting Kristen like a glowing suit of armor was gone, but she was still airborne. All of them were staring at the remains of Chimera Overkill. The loss was a double one for Chris. He had spent so much time in Chimera Overkill, linked to her systems, that she had in many ways been a part of him. The loss of Caroline stung him greater though. Somehow, he couldn't quite believe she was gone.

"Uh, guys!" Prince's voice rang out of the comm. "A little help, please!"

Cygnus Rush was still engaged with the last of the demons, a massive armadillo-like monster, and on the run from it. Prince's super mecha had never been designed for close combat. Cygnus Rush was basically a walking missile launcher. In such close proximity to her enemy, her only means of close in defense was the Gatling guns mounted on her arms or hand-to-hand melee combat. And the Gatling guns were having no effect at all on the heavily armored demon. The rounds that spewed out of them sparked against the monster's shell and ricocheted off of it.

Still reluctant to use Omega Ridder's massive particle cannon, Chris choose a different tactic. Omega Ridder ran several steps forward and then launched herself back into the air. She flew like a guided missile towards the armadillo demon, scoping it up from behind as her hands grabbed the beast under its arms. The armadillo demon struggled against her hold on it but couldn't find the leverage to break free. Omega Ridder soared upwards through the clouds and beyond them. Chris shouted in glee as she burst into space. The armadillo continued to try to tear free of her hold on it as Omega Ridder began to spin, picking up speed with each turn, and then hurled the giant demon away from the Earth, outward into space towards the stars.

Level One completed, the game informed Chris. *Level Two commencing in ten ... nine ...*

Realigning Omega Ridder for a fast decent, Chris poured on the power as he raced to rejoin the others before the game's voice finished its countdown. The air burned as flames ignited and licking at Omega Ridder as she descended through the atmosphere. Chris kept pushing her as the voice continued to count.

Six ... Five ... Four ...

Chris spotted the others. He could see Brannon inside Furious Thunder's pilot compartment as the top of the super mecha's head was gone. The two Hexers still flew about the damaged mecha as if keeping watch over Brannon. Cygnus Rush was damaged as well, but she hadn't taken anywhere near the level of beating that Furious Thunder had. All of them were watching him as Omega Ridder landed near them.

Two ... One ... the game voice chanted inside Chris's mind.

"Be ready for anything!" Chris shouted over Omega Ridder's comm to the others.

Level 2 commencing...

An unexpected voice answered him. It belonged to Colonel Mal.

"You betrayed us, Avalon! You left New Busan to burn!" Mal raged at him as Midnight Blighter and the other super mecha of Reaper Squad emerged from a newly open dimensional portal from the direction that the Nexus lay in. Midnight Blighter came through it first, all gleaming black armor, a walking metal incarnation of death. Skull Tank followed next, the massive head that made up the body atop its tank-like treads giving an eternally feral grin. Then came Shrieking Banshee, a purple-hued super mecha with sonic-based weapons affixed to its shoulders. The portal closed behind them as Reaper Squad moved to engage to them.

Chris didn't know if they were real or merely constructs created by the demonic energy surrounding the Nexus, but he felt like he had to give them the benefit of the doubt.

"We had no choice, Mal!" Chris shouted back at Colonel Mal. "Using the power of the Nexus against the demons is the only way to stop them."

"New Busan is gone, Avalon!" Mal continued to rage. "It fell hours after you left it to die! The demons broke through the Defense Grids. They overran the city, killing everyone they found. General Aketo died in his office, gutted and eaten by those monsters!"

Chris thought of Jordon and felt sick. What had the demons done to her? Surely she was dead too if this was the real Colonel Mal. He tried to remind himself that all of Ki-land was nothing more than a game, and once he and the others reached the Nexus, everything would be okay again as the entire world was rebooted and reset, free of the taint of the demons. It was a hard thing to do. Ki-land was more real to him than his life outside it, and his love for Jordon wasn't just acting out the part of his character in the game.

"You don't want to do this, Mal!" Chris warned.

"Reaper Squad, take them out!" Colonel Mal ordered.

"For New Busan!" Anna, Shrieking Banshee's pilot, screamed.

Skull Tank opened fire first, the energy beams of its eyes slashing through the night at Cygnus Rush. Master Travi and Kristen flew between Cygnus Rush and the incoming blast of energy, conjuring a shield in front of the super mecha together. Skull Tank's eyebeams struck the shield, crackling and burning against it. The shield cracked, but it held.

Shrieking Banshee charged Furious Thunder. Furious Thunder limped forward to meet her but never got the chance to engage the Reaper Squad mecha. Shrieking Banshee came to a skidding halt as it unleashed a howl the shook Furious Thunder's body. Exposed but still strapped in the Furious Thunder's damaged pilot compartment, Brannon had no protection from the sonic waves that crashed into the super mecha. His body exploded into a mass of bloody pulp that stained the remaining walls of Furious Thunder's pilot compartment. Furious Thunder's giant body slumped over as Anna cackled with laughter.

Omega Ridder and Midnight Blighter circled like a pair of boxers, each looking for an opening in which to strike. Chris still had Omega Ridder's wrist blades extended. He could tell Colonel Mal wanted this fight to be an up close and personal one because Midnight Blighter twirled a black-bladed battle axe in its hands. Energy crackled and danced like living lightning over the axe's blade.

"I've waited a long time for this, Avalon," Colonel Mal told him.

"This is madness, Mal. We should be working together," Chris pleaded. "We can still save New Busan and all of Ki-land. The Nexus holds to the key to everything. Can't you see that?"

"The only thing I want to see, Avalon, is your soul burning in the fires of Hell," Mal spat as Midnight Blighter rushed forward swinging its axe in a wide arc at Omega Ridder.

Sparks flew, and a clang as loud as a sonic boom rang out as Omega Ridder parried Midnight Blighter's swing with her right arm blades. Midnight Blighter heaved the axe back with unexpected speed to strike at her again. This time, Omega Ridder side stepped Midnight Blighter's attack as Chris slashed at the enemy super mecha with an attack of his own. The blades of Omega Ridder's left arm punctured the thick, black armor of Midnight Blighter's side. Chris gave them a twist before yanking them free. Midnight Blighter stumbled, sparks flying from the super mecha's damaged entrails as smoke rolled out of the mess the blades had made of its side.

"Give it up, Mal," Chris said. "Midnight Blighter is no match for me in this thing."

Mal's cackling laughter reeked of madness as Midnight Blighter recovered raising its axe once more. "You're not the only one who has gotten some upgrades, Avalon."

Midnight Blighter's chest split open as a trio of large barrels slid out from inside it. They all fired in a simultaneous concussion of noise. The unexpected move caught Chris utterly by surprise. Even as fast as Omega Ridder was, there was no time to dodge. The first of the three missiles covered in black, mystical energy that arced about them during their flight towards Omega Ridder struck her shoulder. It blew away a chunk of her armor there. Chris, linked to the new super mecha on a whole other level than he had been to Chimera Overkill, screamed in pain. Omega

Ridder's left hand jerked up to catch the second missile before it impacted against her chest. It exploded in her grip, tearing her hand apart. The third missile struck Omega Ridder full on, leaving a gaping, smoking hole in her chest armor as she collapsed, toppling over to thud to the ground on her back. Chris grunted as the safety straps that kept him in his pilot seat cut into him. He felt one of his ribs snap, gritting his teeth at the pain inside his chest.

Cygnus Rush, saved by the two Hexers, returned fire at Skull Tank. The giant head's treads tossed masses of earth skyward as its pilot must have realized that he or she had no real hope against Cygnus Rush in a long-range battle. Skull Tank sped away as missiles exploded around it, some striking the path ahead of it, others the path behind. Still others detonated in the air near the grinning monstrosity of the face that was the bulk of its body. Skull Tank was pouring the power of its reactor into Electronic Counter Measures in order to misdirect Cygnus Rush's fire and stay alive. Cygnus Rush's ineffective barrage continued as Skull Tank ran of its life.

One of Shrieking Banshee's hands reached out to shove the broken and off-line remains of Furious Thunder over. Shrieking Banshee turned, setting its sight on Cygnus Rush, its sonic weapons powering up for another blast as Master Travi and Kristen came swooping in. Beams of energy from Master Travi's hands sliced across the weapon mounted on the super mecha's right shoulder while Kristen assaulted the one on its left. The weapon Master Travi had targeted during his flyby blew taking a good chunk of Shrieking Banshee's shoulder along with it. Shards of fractured armor spun away from the fire that raged violently in the spot where the weapon had been located. Kristen's attack was weaker than Master Travi's. Her energy beams appeared to do little more than melt sections of the armor plating that protected

Shrieking Banshee's the weapon mounted on the super mecha's left shoulder.

Shrieking Banshee whirled about, tracking the two Hexers as they sped away from it. Its pilot attempted to fire the super mecha's left sonic weapon at the Hexers. The power built within the weapon but didn't discharge. Instead, the weapon overloaded and blew apart in a similar fashion to the one Master Travi had destroyed. Shrieking Banshee staggered to the right as its left shoulder blew apart and its left arm fell from its body, severed by the blast.

As Shrieking Banshee recovered and the two Hexers came in for another run it, a mouth dilated open below the super mecha's blazing red eyes. The scream that came out of its mouth washed over the two Hexers. Master Travi swerved about in the air, his hands covering his ears despite the protection afforded to him by the magical shield about his body. Kristen, her shield already weakened, died instantly. Her clothes were shredded and the very flesh stripped from bones by the sheer intensity of the force that tore at her.

Master Travi's flight arced upwards as managed to find control of it again. The master Hexer sped skyward out of the cone of Shrieking Banshee's continuing cry. Once clear of it, Master Travi hung in the air as he prepared a new spell.

Shrieking Banshee struggled to turn its head upwards to the height where the master Hexer floated. It couldn't do it though. The servo motors of the joints in Shrieking Banshee's neck had been taken hits on both sides from its exploding shoulders.

Master Travi trapped in the depths of his power, summoning it all forth to be used against the super mecha in a single blast. As his chanting reached its crescendo, the master Hexer aimed both of his hands at Shrieking Banshee, unleashing the power he had gathered. The discharge from Master Travi's open palms was brighter than the midday sun and lit the night like detonating mega flare. Shrieking Banshee blew apart in an explosion that lit the night a second time. In the wake of the second flash, all that remained of Shrieking Banshee were bits and pieces of burnt and slagged metal scattered across the fields where it had once stood. Spinning downward like an out-of-control jet fighter, Master Travi crashed to the earth. His body was pulped and splattered over the grass around where it struck the ground.

Omega Ridder rolled to her feet as shook off the pain he was feeling and brought her back into the fight. Midnight Blighter was almost upon her, its battle axe raised to strike the final blow. Chris kicked Omega Ridder's flight engines up to full and she soared skyward as the blade of Midnight Blighter's axe slashed through the now empty space where she had once stood.

Midnight Blighter's head craned upwards as Colonel Mal shouted, "You coward! Come back down here and see this fight through with honor!"

"What would you know of honor?" Chris snorted as Omega Ridder reached to draw her particle cannon.

Chris imagined he saw the gleaming yellow eyes of Midnight Blighter go wide as he targeted the leader of Reaper Squad with Omega Ridder's particle cannon and squeezed the weapon's trigger. The shot it fired was beyond anything Chris had ever imagined being possible. The shot vaporized Midnight Blighter where it stood and then dug into the earth, slicing downwards through miles upon miles of dirt and rocks and then magma. The concussive shockwave of the weapon's beam striking the earth spread outward like the blossoming blast of a MOAB. Skull Tank was close enough to the blast's epicenter to be picked up and hurled along with the debris the shockwave carried. Cygnus Rush had time to brace for the shockwave's impact, falling to one knee and bringing its arms up and together like a shield in front of its body. Even so, the shockwave swept Cygnus Rush from her feet and flung her backwards like a toy being cast away by an angry child. Cygnus Rush bounced and rolled over the fields of farmland before finally coming to a stop.

Omega Ridder descended slowly from the sky, her feet touching down on the scorched earth. She stood there as Chris stared in awe at the level of destruction he had wrought as coils of smoke leaked from the barrel of the particle cannon Omega Ridder clutched.

Level 2 completed! the game's voice intruded upon his thoughts. *Plane shift required for level 3 activation. Engaging ...*

The world around Omega Ridder rippled and changed. Suddenly, the hulking super mecha was no longer standing in the fields of the American heartland. She and Cygnus Rush were transported somewhere *else*. Farmlands and fields became a sea of glittering crystals.

Cygnus Rush pushed herself to her feet as Prince said, "Where are we, Colonel?"

"We're inside the Nexus," Chris answered as Omega Ridder shouldered her massive weapon and one of her hands reached out to point at the sun-like orb that floated several miles above the crystalline sea ahead of them. "That's the heart of all of Ki-land."

"We've made it then." Prince sounded relieved though his tone was tinged with sadness. "Kristen and the others would have loved to see this place."

Level 3 beginning in ten ... nine ... eight ...

"Do you hear that voice?" Prince asked. "Or is just inside my head? It's talking about some level starting."

"You can hear it?" Chris was stunned.

"I do," Prince confirmed as the voice droned on.

Four ... Three ..

"What does it mean, sir? Are we losing our minds?" Prince was totally freaked out.

"Don't worry about the voice, Prince," Chris told him. "Worry about that thing instead."

Level 3 commencing ...

A great tentacle mass came rolling towards them from underneath the Nexus. Either it had just been brought into existence or it had somehow been hiding itself from their perception of it before. Chris didn't suppose it mattered. It was showing itself now and clearly wanted them both dead.

The thing was larger than both of the super mecha put together. And it was as monstrous as it was large. Slime smeared the barbed lengths of its tentacles as they slashed wildly about in the air and it sped along with an impossible seeming speed.

"Oh screw this," Chris muttered and raised Omega Ridder's particle cannon at the ball of tentacles. Omega Ridder fired. The blast from the particle cannon sent bits of tentacles spinning through the air and black blood splattered over the crystalline ground.

Everything was silent and still as Chris stared across the crystalline sea at the Nexus in the distance.

"That was too easy," Prince said.

"Tell me about it," Chris snorted. "I got a feeling that thing was just the beginning of what we're going to face here."

"Yeah about that ..." Prince quipped. "Where exactly is here anyway?"

"The Nexus," Chris answered as Omega Ridder stored her cannon away on her back in order for it be recharged by the reactor that powered her.

"That tells me absolutely nothing, Colonel," Prince complained.

"Look, I don't really know anything more than you do, Prince," Chris lied. "We must be on some kind of other plane of reality. That voice was talking about a 'plane shift' before everything blinked out and we found ourselves here."

"The Nexus is impossible for us to destroy," Chris said. "But it can be damaged. If we do enough damage to it, it'll cease to exist for a split second while it reforms itself. Everything around us, planet Earth, all of reality will blink out with it and be changed like the Nexus itself when it returns. Do you understand, Prince? When it heals itself, it will heal everything else along with it. Everything will be set back to normal, the way it was before the demons came."

"I'm not going to pretend to understand any of that, Colonel, but I'll follow your lead." Cygnus Rush's head nodded as Prince added, "Just like I always have, sir."

"So human, you have come!" a voice like thunder, but not one belonging to Ki or any of the A.I.'s subprograms Chris had ever heard before, laughed. "And one of your little friends even made it here with you."

Omega Ridder and Cygnus Rush turned around towards the source of the voice. A shape was forming from the very crystals that composed the ground they stood on. It took on a humanoid shape as it grew to stand three hundred feet tall. The being flexed its neck and then raised its hands before its glowing blue eyes to watch its fingers as it curled and uncurled them.

"Who are you?" Chris asked.

"If you refer to the monsters that run loose in Ki-land as demons, then I think it fit that you should call me Baal," the crystalline entity answered.

"You're the source of the infection that has tainted everything here," Chris muttered.

"Yes, Chris," the entity laughed. "And I am like you. I still have a body in the world outside of Ki-land too. It's rotting like all the other poor souls who died logged in the game, but I no longer have need of it so that doesn't matter."

Chris sensed there was much more to what the entity had just said than was apparent. "What do you mean you don't need it anymore? Why? Is I because you intend to stay here forever like I'm planning to do after I kick your sorry butt?"

The entity laughed again. "You're not shocked to find there is another human still alive in this game?"

"You just said you were dead and I know you were infected when you died. You were the first to carry the plague here to this world," Chris reminded the crystalline creature. "I don't think that means you can count yourself as human any longer."

"I said my body was rotting Chris," the crystal monster corrected him. "Not that I was dead. I live on here as my new body is being constructed out there."

Chris was stunned beyond the ability of speech. He didn't doubt for a second that the monster he now faced was a Player Character like himself or at least a self-aware, computer generated remnant of one.

"And where are you building this body?" Chris asked, curious.

"Aboard the Orb, of course, my dear colonel," the entity answered him. "There is nowhere else remaining that has the power and tools to create such a construct."

Chris's blood ran cold in his veins. "The Orb?" he repeated.

"I have been for some time," the entity mocked him.

"That's impossible," Chris stammered.

"Is it?" The entity's crystal lips moved like they were made of organic tissue to smirk at him. "I am very grateful that you saved us both from the debris that recently struck the Orb, Chris. For that, you have my thanks."

The crystalline creature shook its head sadly. "But even so, I can't allow you to live. The real world as we both knew it is gone. It lies in flames and ashes. We are the last two souls that remain from all those that dwelled upon the Earth. I have evolved and become something far greater than the man I was. You have not. You cling to ideas and beliefs that died with our race while I look to the future and what it holds for myself and the children I will create to populate it."

"You're insane," Chris muttered.

"Am I?" the entity asked. "You could join me, Chris, rule the new world that is to be, but I know you won't. It's not in you. You don't have the stomach to let go of the past and embrace change as it was meant to be."

"Uh, sir ..." Prince spoke up over Omega Ridder's comm. "What in the holy, fragging devil are you two talking about? Is that thing saying Ki-land isn't real, that all of this is just game?"

Omega Ridder's head nodded as Chris said, "I'm sorry, Prince, but that part is true."

"I ... I'm not alive?" Prince stammered.

"I didn't say that," Chris started but before he could say anything, Prince cut him off.

"So Kristen, Caroline, all the others? My family even? None of them were ever real?" Prince raged. "All this is just a made up fantasy?"

The crystalline entity was shaking with laughter. "Oh little my precious little NPC, what a glorious time it is for you to learn the truth of things. It must hurt to know that you don't matter, that you've never mattered, little one."

"Colonel," Prince said, "can we just stop talking now and kill that thing already?"

"I'd say it's time." Chris smiled inside Omega Ridder's pilot seat, filled with pride at Prince's determination to finish the job they had started together and sacrificed so many friends and relationships for in order to see through. "You take out the Nexus. I'll deal with this mother."

The crystalline entity was still laughing as Omega Ridder popped her arm blades and lunged towards it as he noticed the plane shift had also repaired all the damage Midnight Blighter had done to her. Cygnus Rush ran for a closer firing position as Prince began to target the glowing mass that was the core of the Nexus.

Omega Ridder's blades slammed into the crystalline entity's chest. Chips of shattered crystal flew as the blades of her right arm sparked against it. The crystal entity, unmoved by his attack, backhanded Omega Ridder. The force of the blow shook Chris inside her pilot compartment as Omega Ridder was knocked from her feet and sent flying. She never touched the ground though. Chris activated her flight systems and she soared upwards into the sky.

"Impressive suit you have there," the entity snickered at Chris as Omega Ridder continued to gain altitude. "Not that it will save you."

The entity raised a hand towards Omega Ridder. Shards of crystal flew from its fingers like machine gun rounds flickering in the light of the Nexus as they streaked through the air. Omega Ridder broke hard to the right, dodging them. Chris cursed at just how close they had come despite the speed the super mecha was moving at.

Unbothered that it had missed, the entity watched Omega Ridder come to a stop in the sky above it as the super mecha drew her particle cannon. Omega Ridder leveled the barrel of the weapon at the entity and squeezed the trigger. The crystalline entity made no move to dodge the incoming blast. It stood where it was and allowed the blast to strike it. The blast from the particle cannon hammered into the entity and broke apart, redirected like rays of light being scattered by a prism. Omega Ridder found herself dodging her own blast as several of the rays were hurled back towards her.

Out of the corner of his eye, Chris noticed that Cygnus Rush stood before the Nexus. He imagined Prince was running scans on it, trying to figure out how best to destroy it. His attention snapped back to the battle he was engaged in as the crystalline entity's arms stretched upwards, elongating to grab at him. Crystal fingers closed around both of Omega Ridder's ankles as the entity jerked the super mecha out of the sky. It slammed Omega Ridder into the ground with such force that Chris nearly blacked out from the shockwave the impact sent through the super mecha's body. Omega Ridder's particle cannon bounced from her hands. The entity released the super mecha, making a lunge for the weapon. It swept up the particle cannon and twisted the middle of the weapon. Metal bent and tore apart beneath the pressure of its crystal fingers before the weapon exploded. Its power core ruptured. The ensuing explosion left the entity without its arms and hands. Its chest and upper legs were badly damaged and splintered as well. Staggering, the entity glared at Omega Ridder as Chris recovered and brought the super mecha to its feet.

"Enough of this," the entity told him. It sprang at Omega Ridder, changing as it rushed forward. By the time it reached the super mecha, it was no longer made of crystal. The crystalline entity had assumed what was likely its true form. Giant, leathery wings sprouted from its back. Its arms regrew into masses of whipping tentacles. The crystal of its body was gone, replaced by slime-slicked, green scales. Its eyes were open, roaring flames out of which black smoke poured, rising upwards over its wide forehead.

Omega Ridder braced herself as the entity's new form crashed into her, knocking her over and taking her to the ground beneath it. Tentacles ripped and tore at Omega Ridder's armor as a tongue with a spear-like tip shot from its mouth to plunge towards her head. Chris jerked Omega Ridder's head to the side just in time to avoid it being impaled by the monster's tongue. Omega Ridder's powerful arms strained, their servo motors screaming, as he tried to force the monster off of her.

"Colonel!" Prince's voice called to him over Omega Ridder's comm. "I've finally got a lock on the Nexus's core, sir."

"Take the shot!" Chris yelled. "Take it now!"

The burning eyes of the creature looked up at where Cygnus Rush stood in horror.

"No!" the entity howled as Cygnus Rush opened fire with everything she had. Every one of her numerous launchers emptied their payloads of missiles into the Nexus. Explosions bubbled outward from inside the Nexus as Cygnus Rush's missile flew to detonate within its center.

The Nexus shrank inward upon itself and then blew apart in a flash of light and energy that washed over everything. The energy of the blast spread across all of Ki-land, erasing everything in its path, like a great nothingness swallowing up all of reality.

In the span of a few seconds, an entire world died.

****

Chris came awake with a start inside of Omega Ridder. Her systems were offline and he struggled to bring them back up. Without her sensors and tactical display, he was basically blind. All he could see through the slit of her visual viewport was darkness. It took him several minutes to get her sensors functional and he breathed a sigh of relief as her tactical display came back into being in front of his eyes.

Omega Ridder floated in a void of nothingness. The entity's body floated opposite her, its burning eyes closed. He knew it wasn't dead though. Smoke still leaked from the corners of its closed eyelids. As he stared at the entity, wondering how and why the two of them hadn't been erased along with the rest of Ki-land, those eyes fluttered open. The fires within them burned brightly with rage.

"You ..." the entity growled in fury. "You've destroyed everything."

"I did what had to be done," Chris said.

Full system reboot in progress ... full system reboot in progress ... the voice of Ki, the game's A.I., kept repeating over and over.

"When Ki-land comes back online, you'll have no place in it, demon," Chris told the entity. "Ki will be able to send you back into the real world and deny you access forevermore."

"Such dramatic language, little man," the entity snapped at him. "Did it ever occur to you that I might have prepared for this? There was always a chance you might succeed in rebooting the system. I was never fool enough to believe otherwise."

Disengaging all player character neural links ... disengaging ... Ki's voice droned. System reboot in progress ... system reboot in progress.

"I'll see you on the other side, Chris," the entity laughed.

Chris's eyes bugged as he remembered what the demon had told him of its plans and where it was building the new body for itself in the real world as his neural link into Ki-land was severed. He fell through the void, toppling head over heels. Omega Ridder was gone now and he was on his own against the monster.

****

Chris's real body arced as he came awake, sucking in a deep breath of fear. His hands slammed against the transparent canopy of his game interface chamber, shoving it open. He knew he had to be in shock as he grabbed the chamber's side and heaved himself over its edge to flop onto the metal floor of the Orb. Somewhere on the station, the entity would be waking up too. He knew it as surely as he knew that he was dead if he didn't arm himself quickly. His entire body trembled as he used the side of the chamber to pull himself up to his feet. His legs were refusing to properly respond to the commands his brain was sending them. He had been inside of Ki-land for a very long time. In his reflection upon the canopy of the game chamber, he saw the beard that had grown to cover the lower half of his face. He felt so weak, but there was nothing for it. There was no time. He had to roll the hard six.

Stumbling along, Chris used the wall of the gaming area for support as he got himself moving and tried to get his body working properly again. By the time he reached the exit door that led out into the Orb's winding corridors, he was beginning to feel better. He could only hope that the entity was having just as much trouble readjusting to the real world as he was.

Chris paused at the door to use the data panel on the wall next to it. "Computer, run a scan of the station for any anomalous activity or power drains."

"Power drain in section 12B, engineering," the Orb's computer told him.

Good, Chris thought. That put an entire deck between him and whatever the entity was becoming in the real world. If it was still draining power, maybe whatever body it had been constructing for itself wasn't fully online yet. Chris, his legs finally beginning to feel stable again, broke into a full-out run as he left the gaming area behind, sprinting through the corridor. The Orb's armory wasn't far and he had to reach it as fast as he could. His legs pumped beneath him becoming stronger and surer with each step.

Chris skidded to a stop outside the armory and reached to into the access code that would open its locked blast doors. His fingers flew over the key of the door's panel. A moment later, the armory doors slid open before him. He stared into the depths of the Orb's armory. It wasn't a large room. There wasn't much of need for personal weapons in space and the armory's contents were limited. He knew he was going to need as much firepower as he could get his hands on though. He walked into the armory and grabbed one of the four automatic shotguns that hung on its wall and then popped open a case of shells, loading the weapon. Once the shotgun was loaded and he had shoved a handful of extra shells and pre-loaded magazines into the pocket of his uniform, he looked around the room for anything else he thought might be of use. He didn't bother with any of the armory's handguns. Chris figured whatever body the creature had made of itself would be too powerful for them to have much effect on.

His training for his time on the Orb wasn't combat based. He had never been part of the station's security even when there had been a crew abroad it. He didn't know crap about making bombs, but he knew he needed some explosives. There were no grenades or their like to be had, but there were some blasting charges stored in the armory because it was the safest place to keep them. He snatched up two of them, trying to remember what he knew about using them. Their detonators were timer based, that much he did know. He smiled as an idea occurred to him and he set about making it a reality.

Geared up as best as he could be, Chris left the armory and emerged into the Orb's corridors again, determined to go out fighting. He paused to check on the power drain in section 12B via a panel on the corridor's wall. The power drain had ceased two minutes earlier, according to the Orb's computer. That meant the demon could be anywhere by now. He had no idea how fast it was, how strong it was, or anything about what form the entity had created for itself in the real world. All he knew was that it was time to slay a monster.

Chris figured the entity would head for the station's control room. If it reached there ahead of him, it could use the Orb's sensors to locate him. After that, it would be a simple matter of venting the air out of whatever section of the station he was in at the time and the human race would end with him. Rationally, he realized the human race was dead anyway. He wasn't immortal, and there was no one else to make babies with. There were no future generations ahead for mankind. It would die with him no matter the outcome of the battle ahead of him. But, that didn't mean humanity had to end today. It wasn't in his nature to give up and certainly didn't intend to. Humanity and its legacy would live on Ki-land, he told himself. With the system rebooted and Ki restored, there was hope, or at least the fantasy of it.

As Chris raced for the bridge, a song erupted over the Orb's internal comm. system.

"All the people that died, died!" some singer's voice rang out. The song had a fast beat and Chris thought he recognized it from some old horror film.

Chris snorted at the song's happy beat and morbidly dark lyrics. Somehow, it seemed fitting. He rounded a corner in the corridor and found himself facing the door to the Orb's control room. Then he saw it. The entity was coming towards the door along the corridor opposite from where he stood. Its metal feet clanged against the metal floor of the corridor with each step it took. The entity's new body stood roughly seven feet tall. It didn't appear as if the entity had the time to fully complete it. It was a metal mockery of the human form. The body had the two legs and arms of a human but two smaller arms protruded from its sides. Wires ran over its metal frame and its eyes shined with an electric shade of red. Upon seeing him, the entity extended one of its three-fingered hands. Their claw-like tips raked along the side of the corridor it walked through, rending the metal of the walls beneath them.

"Little man," the entity snorted, "you just don't know when to surrender, do you?"

Bringing the butt of the automatic shotgun he carried up to be braced against his shoulder, Chris opened fire. The shotgun bucked in his hands as he hosed the creature with its entire magazine of shells. Sparks flew as the blasts smashed into the entity's body and the thunder of the blasts echoed in the corridor. The entity reeled backwards from their impact. Chris couldn't tell if they had actually hurt the monster though.

"I made this body to be immortal, little man," the entity growled. "Do you truly think you can do more than slow me down?"

Chris lowered the empty shotgun, popping its spent magazine and digging a fresh one from the pockets of his uniform. His nerves got the best of him. The adrenaline coursing through him made his movements too fast and he dropped the magazine he had been trying to shove into the shotgun. It clattered to land at his feet.

The entity's hulking metal body lunged forward like a great predatory cat moving with unexpected speed. Chris threw himself to the floor as the claws of its right hand slashed through where he had just been standing. Rolling, Chris came to his feet behind the metal monster, putting as much distance between himself and it as possible. He'd lost his shotgun. He watched as one of the entity's feet came down on the weapon, shattering it.

"What now?" the entity demanded of him. "Does it not make more sense to accept your fate than to keep up this charade of a fight?"

Chris laughed. "You keep telling yourself that, you bastard."

Reaching behind his back, Chris retrieved the small bundle tucked in his belt there.

"I made this just for you." Chris grinned. "I hope you like it."

Chris hurled the bundle at the monster. It clanged against the metal of the entity's chest and stuck there. The entity looked down at it in confusion.

"Magnets, you mother—" Chris started but never got to finish as the timer of the charges he had strapped together in the bundle reached zero. The blast knocked Chris from his feet. Pieces of debris from the entity's exploding body embedded themselves in his flesh and others cut at his cheeks, arms, and legs. The world seemed to spin about him as he thudded onto the floor.

As he shuddered, fighting against the pain of his numerous wounds, Chris's blood-smeared hand reached for the device on the side of his head, covered by his hair. His fingers stroked at it trying to activate it as he took his final breath and his eyes fell closed.

****

Chris rolled over in bed, reaching out for Jordon. His hand found her thigh and came to rest gently upon it. She stirred at his touch, snuggling closer to him.

"Good morning, lover," she whispered in the dim starlight that leaked into the bedroom through the window across from the bed they shared.

Her voice was like that of an angel, the smell of her hair filling Chris with a heavenly bliss.

"Good morning," he whispered back at her, sliding his hand up along the curves of her body to embrace her and pull her closer to him still.

Chris didn't know if the remote entrance to the game world of Ki-land had worked or if he had died and entered heaven, but he didn't care. Either way, he was with Jordan. That was all that mattered. The future looked bright, and he was sure there many wonderful days ahead of him yet.

END

Read on for a free sample of Total Immersion: Dark World

Author Bio

Eric S Brown is the author of numerous book series including the Bigfoot War series, the Kaiju Apocalypse series (with Jason Cordova), the Crypto-Squad series (with Jason Brannon), the Homeworld series (With Tony Faville and Jason Cordova), the Jack Bunny Bam series, and the A Pack of Wolves series. Some of his stand alone books include War of the Worlds plus Blood Guts and Zombies, World War of the Dead, Last Stand in a Dead Land, Sasquatch Lake, Kaiju Armageddon, Megalodon, Megalodon Apocalypse, Kraken, Alien Battalion, The Last Fleet, and From the Snow They Came to name only a few. His short fiction has been published hundreds of times in the small press in beyond including markets like the Onward Drake and Black Tide Rising anthologies from Baen Books, the Grantville Gazette, the SNAFU Military horror anthology series, and Walmart World magazine. He has done the novelizations for such films as Boggy Creek: The Legend is True (Studio 3 Entertainment) and The Bloody Rage of Bigfoot (Great Lake films). The first book of his Bigfoot War series was adapted into a feature film by Origin Releasing in 2014. Werewolf Massacre at Hell's Gate was the second of his books to be adapted into film in 2015. Major Japanese publisher, Takeshobo, recently bought the reprint rights to his Kaiju Apocalypse series (with Jason Cordova) and it is slated for 2018 release in Japan. Ring of Fire Press will be releasing a collected edition of his Monster Society stories (set in the New York Times Best-selling world of Eric Flint's 1632) later this year. In addition to his fiction, Eric also writes an award winning comic book news column entitled "Comics in a Flash." Eric lives in North Carolina with his wife and two children where he continues to write tales of the hungry dead, blazing guns, and the things that lurk in the woods.

WELCOME TO MY OBSESSION.

I never get sick of the intro cutscene to Elora Online. Headband on, and then fifteen seconds of the most wicked graphics and exciting immersion in the greatest epic of battles, with *Ananta* causing complete mayhem. And damn if he doesn't look cool as hell.

Ananta is controlled by a Nuudle Mystic who summons him. He comes out of the little Nuudle's heart as a swirling blue mist, and then quickly gains form, floating in the air before him.

Ananta is massive. He fills the screen in defined, scaly detail.

He's blue, with nine snake heads that make up most of his body, which is that of a long, forked-tailed serpent. The eyes on the heads have glowing lightning bolts shooting out of them in sparks of silver. Their mouths are enormous, sharp-toothed, and open with hunger only flesh can appease. Surrounding *Ananta* is an aqua fog with black, wispy shadows dancing within. At his outer glow, water droplets spray in a mist.

An army of all races and classes stands before the Mystic and *Ananta*. One green, especially gnarly Mylop lizard can't stand it, the waiting. He raises his axe, roars, and makes a mad run at *Ananta*.

That's my PoV, point-of-view, in the cutscene.

Ananta's belly opens a hole and a golden-skinned man's face emerges. He has glowing, white eyes. That's why we all know *Ananta* is a *he*. The Mystic chants words, commanding the beast. *Ananta*'s mouth opens as all the snake heads turn toward our army of Elora, with gaping mouths brewing fireballs, and flames spew out. They are red, black, yellow, orange, blue, green.

I'm the first to get fried. Then, I'm floating above, and I see the army is wiped out, and Elora is slowing burning, city by city, territory by territory.

And now I'm logged in, in game.

I access my item menu and use my Comfort Ring. I'd been so tired last night that I logged out outside Baneswood in the middle of nowhere. I warp back to my home point in Cashmere, where I'm meeting the guys. And Sally, of course. She gets mad when I call her a guy, but she is.

Today is a big day. Today I get my revenge, and I'm confident. I'm ready. I've been working relentlessly toward this day for eleven months since The Seeker jumped me. I haven't told anyone, but today… I can't wait to get to Lucille's Brewery and tell them what I'm about to do.

They'll think I'm mad. I'm not. Maybe I'm a hero, and not the kind above some revenge. The hero who, yes, does it for revenge, but also because so many people would be free. All over Elora. Heroes are complicated.

No, I'm not one. I know deep down. What I am is a gamer who has taken on the biggest challenge in-game I could find because I can't resist. I made my own mission—I will defeat him where everyone else has failed.

CHAPTER 1: THE TELL

I spawn at the Kila Crystal, where I usually keep my home point, in Cashmere on Wet Eyes Isle. It's in the Marana Sea just outside the underwater Siren Territory. My mansion is on the east coast of the isle. Kila Crystals are for getting around faster, and you have to earn accessing them by finding them. Nobody ever knows if they've found all of them. They're also the only places you can set your HP before you get your first home. Otherwise, you go to your graveyard.

Cashmere's where everybody goes to hang out. Maybe because the auction house synchs up to all the capitals' auction houses, or maybe it's the taverns with the best stat boost brews you can get. It's beautiful, right on the water, peaceful, bustling. Everything is gray, moss-covered stone and quaint structures.

I'm a Dragonbane Maniac. Maniacs are hand-to-hand fighters. I gave myself red spikes down my back, three black spikes on my tail, and curling, big, black horns. White hair, dusky smoke skin. Dragonbane were created eons ago when the mad, power-hungry Bane bred humans and dragons into Dragonbane. It's a long story, the history of Bane, his brother Kane, and Dragonbane altogether. Once, there were humans and dragons, but now only Dragonbane.

Maybe it's because it's this day, but I'm reflecting a lot on my character. How I feel like he's the real me. In Elora Online, you must choose a first and last name, no special characters or numbers. I'm Sid Vicious. That's the real me.

Sometimes you see someone running around with just one name. Must be some secret quest, some item, some reward. No info on the wikis. My guildmates and I have speculated on it for ages, among other oddities of this world.

I'm anxious about telling the guys what I'm going to do—take on The Seeker and destroy him. I know I can, but will I choke and come back defeated, with all my loot gone, starting over? It would be mortifying to tell them after I boast my plans. Better keep it subdued. Like it's not the big, huge deal that it is.

I walk the gray cobblestone streets of Cashmere, watching the other players I pass on my way to Lucille's Brewery. The five races are everywhere—Sirens, the lovely ladies of the sea; Nuudles, the little people who are best at black magic; Mylop, the lizard men giants made for tanking; White Elves, best known for their healing and huge, beautiful territory; and Dragonbane, the best damage dealers in the game, in my opinion. You can pick what race and class you want, and each race has race-specific stat boosts when you start, but you get even more of a stat boost of the race-specific kind if you pick a race and class that are made for each other.

And stat boosts are everything.

I'm a level nothing. There are no levels in Elora Online. Everything is item and stat-based. My stats are through the roof, especially my strength, or STR. It's up to 346 now. When The Seeker got me eleven months ago, it was at 278. Every single digit of a stat boost counts. As a Maniac, STR is my most important stat to do the most damage. My two other big stats I work on to get stronger as a Maniac specifically are attack, or ATT as my secondary stat, and CRG, courage, as my third.

There are seven different stats for your character, and even if you don't have much use for stats like mind (MND) as a Maniac, you still work on all seven as you go. The more stats, the more power, the harder you hit, the more damage you can take, the more good loot you can get, especially when you get high enough to start running dungeons. Plus, Attack (ATT) and Defense (DEF) are must-haves we all grind. We get Attack, Defense, Strength (STR), Mind, Intelligence (INT), Concentration (CON), and Courage (CRG). In eleven months, I've gotten them all higher than they were before The Seeker got me. Yeah, I'm a determined man when it comes to righting wrongs done to me. Revenge, indeed. I want it so bad, I have lived for it for almost an entire year.

I enter the brewery. It has wooden tables and chairs, light wood floors, and a long bar with beautiful Siren NPC, non-player character, bartenders. Behind the bar, a large open window looks out at the water. I see my crew sitting at our usual booth, and they wave and call out to me.

"Sid! He's here! What, you sleep late?" says Peter Johnson, my RL, real life, friend, Jacob, who started playing the day I did. We've been friends since we were kids. He's a green Mylop Lancer. But really, he's a social player and crafts all the time. He's rich as hell from it, too. Tells me everything about crafting. I've tried to explain I like farming for cash, but he still geeks out on crafting so much that he can't help but talk to me about it like we are still eight.

"Be there in a minute, gotta get a drink."

A green-haired Siren NPC behind the bar serves me a huge mug of Blue Ice Ale. It costs a pretty penny. I need it today.

I sit with my friends and guildmates at our booth, between Good Deeds (Sally) and Koolio Koolaide. I see Koolio has the same brew I have but not as big.

I can't wait to tell them, but they are in the middle of talking about Koolio's quest for a new special Lord move that was in the update last week. He's a Siren Lord, a tank who uses healing to do his job, and as all Sirens are female, you know we tease him relentlessly. He always has something witty to say or downright puts you in your place in response. He leads the guild—Nowhere Squares, it's called.

I start chugging my drink. I can feel my body's heart pounding in RL. I don't want to interrupt, but at the same time I want to stand on the table and scream it. I chug instead until Sally notices my drink.

"What are you doing a courage stat boost for? And that huge?"

The drink is a CRG stat booster that lasts four hours, and the stat slowly goes down to your usual stat by the end. My base CRG stat is 271, but once the whole drink is in me, it'll be at 325.

"I was wondering that about Koolio, but I've gathered it's the Chain Heal quest. You have to fight a dragon from the past?"

"Yeah, man," Koolio says. "Need the CRG boost so I can have faster moves."

"Good luck."

"I ain't gonna need it." He sticks his forked Siren tongue out at me.

"But why you, Sid?" Sally persists. I know Sally in RL, too. She's a few years younger, a friend of my sister's. "I know your digital expressions. Your eyes are burning redder with every sip of the brew, and you're all twitchy. Spill." She's a Dragonbane Knight, a real hack-and-slasher. Silver scales and white spikes with red hair. Black, twisting horns.

Nottingham Rose, a UK player and a Nuudle The Black, says, "I see it, too. And how much did you spend on that monstrosity of a drink?" The Blacks are the nukers of the game. Black mage, basically, and big damage. He's slow, but excellent in dungeons. Thorough. Nuudles are small, skinny things, a little like gnomes, but they are proportionate. Nottingham has blue skin, long, black hair in a ponytail, and a red glowing spiral on his forehead. His race is well-known for Nuudle Eyes. Big, round, and oh-so-expressive.

The other Nuudle in our group, Raging Rampager, a Stylist class—the buffers basically—who's always dressed in fabulousness, speaks up. "You've been grinding hard since… you know. Your STR stat must be through the roof now with all the quests and missions you've done. What is it now?"

"346." I chug down the last of the blue ale. My red dragon eyes must be like fire.

"Damn, son," says Peter. "You're drinking all that, you're fidgeting, Deeds's sixth sense is kicking in. What's the game plan for today?"

They all stare at me. Now's the time. I pause. I could just not tell them. What if I lose? I'll be so crushed to tell them I'm doing it and then come back a loser.

However, a little gusto from my friends will help just as much as the blue ale.

In a quiet voice, I say, "I'm going after The Seeker today."

Dead silence. And then everyone talking at once. Lots of questions.

The Seeker is a Dragonbane Killer, basically a ninja. Got the Dragonbane stat boost like I did for picking a race and class that naturally go together. He's often invisible. He's black, has black spikes all over, and sports six twisting horns on his black-haired head.

They want to know how I can find him.

"I've been watching him. He has patterns. I've followed message boards of his attacks on other players, and there's a pattern. He picks certain places at certain times. I'm almost positive I know where he'll be in about a half hour. Plus..." I give them a cocky grin. "I got me a Seer Amulet last week."

"Seer Amulet! Where did you get that? Was it a hidden quest?" yells Peter. Players inside peek over at him with curious expressions.

A Seer Amulet, when worn in the necklace slot of my gear, lets me see invisible things, like an invisible Killer who will be outside the Mantle of Bliss in White Elf Territory ready to pick off mage fishers for their stat boosting items so he can sell them on the AH. All the while killing their progress from possibly years of playing, like he did me. Like he's done to many, many good players.

I hear Sally in the guild chat channel. "He's doing it, guys! Sid is going after The Seeker!" I don't get a chance to tell of the treasure map I bought and found it with, all after reading a Nuudle history book in a library in the Temple of Nuudlel. But meh. We've all done that.

"Dammit, Sally, don't tell everyone. It'll get back to him," chides Peter.

It's too late. Nowhere Squares' chat channel explodes with excitement, all the while Koolio and Peter telling them to keep it to themselves. On the down-low.

"When, Sid?" I hear my favorite voice in the guild say. Silvia Diamond, a blonde, pale White Elf Blessed class. Best pure healers in the game. I've had a crush on her for two years, but never had the balls to do anything about it other than join all her dungeon runs and help her with missions and quests. It's made us good friends, but she's not at our booth every morning, is she?

"I just had my CRG boost drink, and if timing's right, I need to hit the Kila Crystal and head to White Elf Territory's Kila

Crystal in the Mantle of Bliss. I'll get him there. He should be lurking outside in the territory somewhere close," I tell her.

"Wow! That's amazing! I'm in the Mantle now. Want me to tele you here? I'll give you something for good luck," Silvia says.

Nottingham raises a blue eyebrow.

"Sure, thanks. That would be great."

"Give me a minute to run out of the Mantle. That is, you said you wanted to be out there, and it'll be quicker that way. I can use Swift Feet and I'll tele you in five. That stat drink will wear off."

"Well, thanks," I say. In RL, my cheeks are warm.

My friends at the table can't stop talking to the guild about it, so I turn off guild chat. It's making me nervous.

I reach up in RL with my right hand and adjust my headband's viewing to 50 percent. Now I see my apartment and the game equal 50-50. I set my character on auto-static movements. Better empty my bladder before all this gets going. I get up from my gaming recliner and walk to the bathroom, turning off my mic as I take a leak. Then back to my seat. I adjust the headset back to 100 percent and turn my mic back on.

I wonder what gift Silvia might have for me. Now my heart is really hammering.

Silvia invites me to a party. I accept. "Thanks, guys. It's time. Silvia invited me, and she's going to tele me."

Sally tilts her Dragonbane head. "You got this, you know it. If anyone can, you can."

"Yeah," says Koolio Koolaide. "You're the best in the guild. I never said that."

I grin at them. I haven't turned guild chat back on, but I hear Silvia in party chat channel. "Hey, Sid. Are you ready?"

"Yeah. Thanks."

Everything goes white, and then beautiful White Elf Territory surrounds me. Rolling, green hills, bushes, flowers everywhere. Small trees with buds and blooms that never die brush the landscape.

Even more beautiful is the image of Silvia Diamond standing before me, still sparkling from using her white magic to get me here. She smiles at me. I smile back.

"You look nervous. Is that why you got off the guild channel?"

"Yeah." I don't want to look nervous in front of her. I want to be a badass that she swoons over.

"Well, I know you have to get to it. Here. A gift." Her long, slender arms wave in the air and pale blue, sparkling light comes out of her hands. She's using a big move, with me as the target.

Silvia Diamond casts Blessing of Inner Peace. Sid will dodge all Special Ability attacks in next battle.

"That's incredible! Thank you so much, Silv." Blessing of Inner Peace, a Blessed's biggest move acquired through a near-impossible quest (I helped her with it), will allow me to dodge all Special Ability attacks in the next fight I have. She won't be able to cast it again for another day. I'm surprised she had been able to cast it at all. "I mean it."

"One more good luck charm," she says, then takes a step toward me. She leans up and kisses me on the cheek. I'd never wanted physical sensation in Elora more than that moment. She leans back down. "Copy the gameplay log, win or lose. I want to read it, and I want you to tell me all about it. Maybe we could go down to Siren Territory and hang out in a sunken ship or something?"

"I'd like that," I tell her.

"Now go. I know you'll defeat him."

I grin at her. She likes me, acting like it's more than friends. Hell, I don't know. Wow, this day gets crazier and crazier.

We say goodbye, and I'm off to lurk behind trees and bushes in Laninga, an area south of the Mantle of Bliss where, according to my research, I will find The Seeker. Thanks to Silvia's tele, it only takes about three minutes to walk there. I don't dare use my Chimera mount. He'd see me a mile away. Once in Laninga, I use a shadow potion and equip my Seer Amulet. The shadow potion will make me invisible, but if The Seeker also has a Seer Amulet, which he must certainly have stolen off someone, he could see me if he has it equipped. I'm gambling he's in true Killer mode, ready to cut people down fast, and for that he'd have a Stealth Choker equipped. I won't be able to examine his gear. He'd know I was there because he'd get a message saying he was being examined. If he is wearing the Stealth Choker, his Sneak Attack move will do devastating damage when he hits his unknowing victim while invisible at first attack.

Still, I stick to the trees.

I see a few players running here and there. None would be his targets. Too low of stats. They wouldn't have anything good. I can tell simply by looking at what they are wearing.

At sea's edge, on the farthest east side of White Elf Territory in Laninga, I see a shadowy figure crouched down by a Nuudle fishing off the edge. As I get closer, I read that the Nuudle's name is Fangs McGore, and his gear tells me he's a Magician. Wealthy, high stats. I can't imagine the jewelry he has on, but I know that's what The Seeker is after. He'll make a killing on the auction house.

A little closer still, and I can finally read the name in light blue above the shadowy figure. *The Seeker*.

I found him.

Adrenaline pounds through me. I think of Silvia's kiss. I'm ready.

Total Immersion: Dark World is out now!!!

CHECK OUT OTHER GREAT SCIENCE FICTION BOOKS

MAUSOLEUM 2069
by Rick Jones

Political dignitaries including the President of the Federation gather for a ceremony onboard Mausoleum 2069. But when a cloud of interstellar dust passes through the galaxy and eclipses Earth, the tenants within the walls of Mausoleum 2069 are reborn and the undead begin to rise. As the struggle between life and death onboard the mausoleum develops, Eriq Wyman, a one-time member of a Special ops team called the Force Elite, is given the task to lead the President to the safety of Earth. But is Earth like Mausoleum 2069? A landscape of the living dead? Has the war of the Apocalypse finally begun? With so many questions there is only one certainty: in space there is nowhere to run and nowhere to hide.

RED CARBON
by D.J. Goodman

Diamonds have been discovered on Mars.

After years of neglect to space programs around the world, a ruthless corporation has made it to the Red Planet first, establishing their own mining operation with its own rules and laws, its own class system, and little oversight from Earth. Conditions are harsh, but its people have learned how to make the Martian colony home.

But something has gone catastrophically wrong on Earth. As the colony leaders try to cover it up, hacker Leah Hartnup is getting suspicious. Her boundless curiosity will lead her to a horrifying truth: they are cut off, possibly forever. There are no more supplies coming. There will be no more support. There is no more mission to accomplish. All that's left is one goal: survival.

CHECK OUT OTHER GREAT SCIENCE FICTION BOOKS

SALVAGE MERC ONE
by Jake Bible

Joseph Laribeau was born to be a Marine in the Galactic Fleet. He was born to fight the alien enemies known as the Skrang Alliance and travel the galaxy doing his duty as a Marine Sergeant. But when the War ended and Joe found himself medically discharged, the best job ever was over and he never thought he'd find his way again.

Then a beautiful alien walked into his life and offered him a chance at something even greater than the Fleet, a chance to serve with the Salvage Merc Corp.

Now known as Salvage Merc One Eighty-Four, Joe Laribeau is given the ultimate assignment by the SMC bosses. To his surprise it is neither a military nor a corporate salvage. Rather, Joe has to risk his life for one of his own. He has to find and bring back the legend that started the Corp.

SERENGETI
by J.B. Rockwell

It was supposed to be an easy job: find the Dark Star Revolution Starships, destroy them, and go home. But a booby-trapped vessel decimates the Meridian Alliance fleet, leaving Serengeti—a Valkyrie class warship with a sentient AI brain—on her own; wrecked and abandoned in an empty expanse of space. On the edge of total failure, Serengeti thinks only of her crew. She herds the survivors into a lifeboat, intending to sling them into space. But the escape pod sticks in her belly, locking the cryogenically frozen crew inside.

Then a scavenger ship arrives to pick Serengeti's bones clean. Her engines dead, her guns long silenced, Serengeti and her last two robots must find a way to fight the scavengers off and save the crew trapped inside her.

SEVEREDPRESS

CHECK OUT OTHER GREAT
SCIENCE FICTION BOOKS

IN PERPETUITY
by Jake Bible

For two thousand years, Earth and her many colonies across the galaxy have fought against the Estelian menace. Having faced overwhelming losses, the CSC has instituted the largest military draft ever, conscripting millions into the battle against the aliens. Major Bartram North has been tasked with the unenviable task of coordinating the military education of hundreds of thousands of recruits and turning them into troops ready to fight and die for the cause.

As Major North struggles to maintain a training pace that the CSC insists upon, he realizes something isn't right on the Perpetuity. But before he can investigate, the station dissolves into madness brought on by the physical booster known as pharma. Unfortunately for Major North, that is not the only nightmare he faces- an armada of Estelian warships is on the edge of the solar system and headed right for Earth!

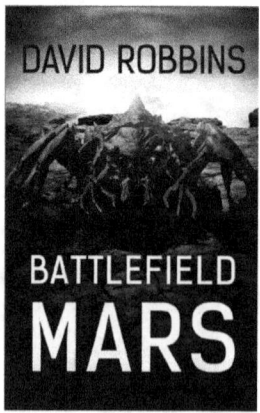

BATTLEFIELD MARS
by David Robbins

Several centuries into the future, Earth has established three colonies on Mars. No indigenous life has been discovered, and humankind looks forward to making the Red Planet their own.

Then 'something' emerges out of a long-extinct volcano and doesn't like what the humans are doing.

Captain Archard Rahn, United Nations Interplanetary Corps, tries to stem the rising tide of slaughter. But the Martians are more than they seem, and it isn't long before Mars erupts in all-out war.

www.ingramcontent.com/pod-product-compliance
Lightning Source LLC
Chambersburg PA
CBHW061248170626
46809CB00007B/2896